HAMLET

IS

NOT

OK

Books by R. A. Spratt

R. A. Spratt

HAMLET IS NOT OK

PENGUIN BOOKS

PENGUIN BOOKS

UK | USA | Canada | Ireland | Australia
India | New Zealand | South Africa | China

Penguin Random House Australia is part of the Penguin Random House group of
companies whose addresses can be found at global.penguinrandomhouse.com.

First published by Penguin Books, an imprint of
Penguin Random House Australia Pty Ltd, in 2023

Cover design by Jessica Cruickshank © Penguin Random House Australia Pty Ltd
Internal design and typesetting by Midland Typesetters, Australia

Printed and bound in Australia by Griffin Press, an accredited
ISO AS/NZS 14001 Environmental Management Systems printer

  A catalogue record for this
book is available from the
National Library of Australia

Penguin Random House Australia uses papers that are natural and recyclable
products, made from wood grown in sustainable forests. The logging and
manufacture processes are expected to conform to the environmental regulations of
the country of origin.

ISBN 978 0 14 377927 8 (Paperback)

penguin.com.au

We at Penguin Random House Australia acknowledge that Aboriginal and Torres
Strait Islander peoples are the Traditional Custodians and the first storytellers of the
lands on which we live and work. We honour Aboriginal and Torres Strait Islander
peoples' continuous connection to Country, waters, skies and communities. We
celebrate Aboriginal and Torres Strait Islander stories, traditions and living cultures;
and we pay our respects to Elders past and present.

I wrote this book during Covid times. When all of us had much more time with our own thoughts. It brought me great joy to sink myself into this world. A world constructed in William Shakespeare's imagination.

So I want to dedicate this book to all the storytellers who bring us joy, comfort and catharsis in turbulent times.

Stories remind us how much of our human experience is shared. The plot points in our lives are constantly happening in distant places and even different times. Hopefully, by continuing to tell stories, we can learn from each other, laugh with each other and comfort each other.

WARNING

This book contains Shakespeare.

Not literally him, the man. That would be impossible (I think). I definitely know that the Royal Shakespeare Trust would be very annoyed with me if I tried to dig up his remains and make them into paper. What I mean is – this book contains bits of text directly quoted from Shakespeare's play *Hamlet*.

In some places, I have weaved the quotes into the dialogue of the book so that it will be easy for you to understand. In other places, I have put the quotes in italics and indented them. These bits are to give you a sense of what Selby (the main character) is reading. It doesn't matter if you don't understand every word (or even any word). It's best to just let the words wash over you, the way you listen to music. If you listen to a pop song on Spotify you don't painstakingly identify every note and chord as you go along. So if you find yourself struggling with the old fashioned vocabulary I recommend this approach.

Now, if you're really, really struggling, you can in fact just skip these indented bits. Get on with enjoying the story of the book. It will make sense without them. You can come back and have a look at them later. You will probably find them easier to understand on a second reading.

I hope you enjoy this book.

Best wishes,
R.A. Spratt

1

Curtain Up

'Imagine you're standing on a castle in Denmark,' said Ms Karim.

This idea caught Selby Michaels' attention. She looked up from her doodling. She wished she was in Denmark. There were so many layers of stories there. It was the home of Vikings. It was the birthplace of Hans Christian Anderson and all the fairy tale characters he created. The legends of the kraken, Thor and all the Norse gods – they all came from that part of the world too. And, of course, Lego. There was so much scope for the imagination there.

Selby tried to visualise Denmark. Her imagination leapt straight to the movie *Frozen*. Which made her think of fjords, which was just a fun word to say with the j sounding like a y. She was itching to say it out loud right now, but she couldn't. The other kids in her class would think she was strange if she started saying 'fjords' in the middle of English class.

Selby looked about her classroom. It was a state school so everything was worn out. The formica on the desks had worn thin because graffiti had been scrubbed off them with super strong solvents so many times. The once-white walls were greying and pock-marked where Blu Tack had come off with chunks of paint. And the lesson plan had been written on the white board with a green marker that didn't quite work. If you were sitting any further back than the third row, there was no way you could read it. Selby wished she could go to Denmark.

She imagined a European forest – like in Hansel and Gretel. A real forest with green trees. Not like her hometown where the trees were more grey than green, and everything was so dry. When you went hiking round her area, there was no time for imagining fictional fairies and goblins. You were too busy keeping a look out for very real snakes.

'Okay, so imagine you're up on that wall,' continued Ms Karim. 'It's night time, so it's spooky, right?'

'Woooooo,' said Ben, one of the sillier boys in the class.

Ms Karim just ignored him. 'When suddenly – the ghost of your father appears before you!'

Isla put her hand up, 'My father isn't dead, miss!'

'We're imagining,' said Ms Karim, valiantly not losing her temper.

'But ghosts aren't real, miss,' Simon called.

'It's a play, we're talking about a play,' snapped Ms Karim, the last remaining thread of her temper had snapped. 'The whole thing is fictional. Reality is what you study in science and history and maths. This is English. We study fiction here. If you can't wrap your mind around that concept, you are going to get very bad marks in your leaving exams.'

Selby looked out the window. She didn't like it when Ms Karim lost her temper and started ranting. It made her feel guilty. Even when she hadn't done anything. Although, usually the problem *was* that she hadn't done anything.

'You think this subject is silly because it's about imagination?' accused Ms Karim. It was a question, but everyone in the class had the sense to realise it was rhetorical, and they should stay quiet. Ms Karim may be only five-foot-one but she was terrifying when she got on a roll. 'You all want to study practical subjects because that's the only thing that will get you a job? Well, I'm here to tell you every job on earth requires problem-solving. The people who get promoted are the people who are good at problem-solving. And problem-solving is all about imagination and creativity. Lateral thinking is your key to success in life.'

Selby glanced at her classmates. She could see they had all tuned out. Ms Karim was right, but there was no point talking to fifteen-year-olds about real life after school. It all seemed so far away. It might as well be fictional too.

Suddenly, the school bell blasted. It was more of a horn than a bell. It was so loud it was impossible to talk over no matter how good a teacher was at voice projection. Everyone started packing up their books and pens.

As soon as the bell fell silent, Ms Karim called out, 'You should be up to act three with your reading.' She had used those three seconds while the bell was sounding to regain her composure. 'Make sure you've finished reading it by tomorrow, so we can discuss Hamlet's motivations in class.'

Everyone groaned. Except Selby. She wasn't going to do the reading. She never did.

Selby Michaels was not a loner by choice. She was just alone because no-one wanted to spend time with her. She was the odd one out. This happens all too easily in a small town when there aren't enough odd people to form your own group.

People liked her well enough. She was polite. She made jokes. She didn't smell bad. There just wasn't anybody else like her. You see, she had all the outward appearance of being a huge nerd, but she wasn't actually good at anything. To be a nerd, you really have to make up for your eccentric behaviour by being a genius at maths, or a prodigy at English, or really good at hacking into Defence Department computers.

This was not Selby. She struggled at school. She couldn't get ideas down on paper without getting herself and her teachers hopelessly confused. She was okay at maths but she hated it. It was so boring, and it always took her three times as long to understand a new concept as it did the other kids.

The worst part was everyone had expected the opposite for her. Selby's parents ran the only bookstore in town. They loved books and words and ideas. Her mother had a master's degree in English literature and her father had given up a career as a geological engineer just so he could run a bookstore – which he did badly, because he was more interested in reading the stock than selling it.

Selby also had an older sister and brother who had excelled at everything. Her sister had been dux of the whole school and was now studying law in the city. Her brother had topped the state in English and Ancient History and won a scholarship to go and study the classics at Durham in England. This left Selby alone at home with her parents, so she could disappoint them all by herself.

Of course, Mr and Mrs Michaels never said they were disappointed. They were really good people. But that was the problem. They were so endlessly encouraging about everything. They so desperately wanted Selby to be a bookworm like everyone else in the family, that if she so much as glanced at a book they would gift it to her. They didn't mind what she read. They'd be happy with anything – romance, graphic novels, action adventure. They even offered to read to her or to buy her audio books. They just wanted her to love books as much as they did. And Selby couldn't be mad about that. She knew it was just because they loved her, and books made them happy and they wanted her to be happy too. But the pressure was crushing.

They'd never gotten angry with her about anything, until now.

It was stocktake time at the bookstore, which was Selby's favourite time of the year, because her parents got so busy at the shop she had lots of time to herself at home. Day after day, her parents worked until seven or eight o'clock at night and Selby loved it. It was a little lonely, but she got to make whatever she wanted for dinner and watch whatever she wanted on TV with no-one to judge her.

Selby had taken to coming home from school and spending two hours watching daytime soap operas. She really enjoyed the ridiculous plots and terrible acting. Then she would make herself dinner, which usually involved baking bread from scratch because there was never enough food in the house. Her parents never prioritised grocery shopping. They ate most of their meals in their own shop. Selby didn't mind being left to sort herself out. She liked cooking.

Then her parents would come home and Selby would go for a walk before bed.

You may have noticed there was something missing from this schedule – homework. If you didn't notice, you're in good company because Selby didn't notice either. She just stopped doing it. And nothing happened. So she forgot about it entirely.

That was until it all went horribly wrong.

It hadn't really occurred to Selby that she was doing anything bad. If anyone found out how she spent her time she would have been embarrassed, because what she was watching on TV was so silly. But it was almost as if the part of her brain that had a conscience when it came to homework had been switched off. That circuit breaker had tripped and no-one had noticed, so no-one had gone to the fuse box to flick it back on.

So it came as a complete surprise to her when her parents returned from the parent-teacher conference at school in a towering rage. She had never seen them so angry before, unless it was with a politician they disagreed with. But this was worse than just anger – it was anger plus disappointment. Anger that she had not done any homework for six months and was now hopelessly behind in every subject, and disappointment that she had deceived them.

This second accusation felt a bit harsh to Selby. She hadn't gone out of her way to deceive them, they just hadn't noticed. But it is often the way that people are angriest with others when they are really angry with themselves, or angry to have been embarrassed themselves. They had been embarrassed to realise, in front of their daughter's English teacher, that they had no idea what Selby had been up to.

'What have you been doing all these months?' asked her mother when they confronted her.

Selby shrugged.

'Really? You don't know?' asked Mum. 'Well I know, because I checked your viewing history on the television.'

'Urgh,' groaned Selby.

'That's it, no more TV, no more computer, no more music, nothing!' yelled her father. 'You come home and you work in the shop until dinner, then you do your homework, study and go to bed.'

Selby sighed. She couldn't argue. It was fair enough. She deserved to be punished.

'Aren't you going to say something!?' demanded Dad. 'You let us down. We trusted you.'

'I'm sorry,' said Selby. But she didn't really sound sorry and her apathy only seemed to make her parents angrier.

'We give you all this freedom,' said Dad. 'We never give you a hard time about school and your bad grades year after year. And in return we get this! Binge watching some brain-dead romance.'

Selby stared at her shoes. She'd hand painted them last year. Her mother hated them. There was an L painted on one and an R painted on the other. She'd done it as a joke. As if she was too stupid to know which foot to put her shoe on. It occurred to her as she stared that if she had really wanted to annoy her mother, she should have painted the L and the R on the opposite shoes. That would have made her mum's inner OCD explode. The longer Selby stared at the shoes, the longer she could go without making eye contact with either of her parents.

'Things have to change,' said her mother. 'This isn't working. You need to do better. We're going to get you a tutor.'

Selby's head snapped up, 'What?'

'Someone to coach you until you catch up on all the work you've missed,' said Mum.

'I can do it myself,' protested Selby.

'You don't have that choice,' said Dad. 'You've proven we can't trust you.'

'The time for hand-holding and patience has gone,' said Mum. 'You need to knuckle down and work hard.'

'Work hard so I can go to university, get a brilliant degree, then run a dilapidated old shop and earn a pittance like you two?' accused Selby. She realised she shouldn't have said it as soon as the words were out of her mouth. But she was a teenager and she had all kinds of hormones coursing through her veins, which is why it's traditional for teenagers to say things that are thoughtless and hurtful.

'Life isn't about money,' said Dad, struggling to control his voice as he simmered with rage. 'There's no shame in having a modest income. There is shame in ignorance – wilful ignorance. A good education is worth more than gold, and it doesn't have to be a degree. It doesn't even have to be high school graduation. It's about a thirst for knowledge, a curiosity to know more. You need to wake up and take responsibility for your own learning.'

'I know stuff,' argued Selby.

'What, like how to kill a duck with a rock?' demanded Mum.

'What?' said Selby.

'Mrs Tink was in the shop this morning,' said Mum. Mrs Tink was an old lady who had lived in the town since before everyone was born. She knew everybody, was related to most people and always knew what was going on. 'She saw you throwing rocks at the ducks in the river.'

'I wasn't doing that,' said Selby. 'I was just throwing rocks in the river.'

'Every day for the last three months?' demanded Mum. 'Did you actually kill any?'

'I wasn't throwing rocks at ducks,' said Selby.

'She saw them flapping away,' said Dad.

'I wasn't aiming for the ducks,' said Selby. 'I may have thrown one that went a bit off target.'

Mum shrugged. 'We can't believe a word you say anymore.'

2

Crime and Punishment

A nd so the next day after school, Selby came straight home because home was the bookstore. They lived in the apartment above the shop. She dropped her bag behind the counter and went to work.

It was not a very busy bookstore at the best of times, but it was particularly quiet in the afternoon. Mum and Dad were still really angry with her, so Mum disappeared down to the back of the store to do stocktaking and Dad took all the deliveries down to the post office to ship. Selby just had to sit at the counter so that passers-by could tell that the shop was open, and shoplifters wouldn't come in and steal anything.

Not that there was a lot of shoplifting in their town. The Venn diagram of the literate community and the type of people who would steal didn't overlap much. Most of the stealing was done by old ladies too embarrassed to be seen buying romance novels, and they wouldn't be put off by a sixteen-year-old sitting at the counter. You'd actually have to insist on looking in their handbag to catch those. Then they'd probably just pretend to have dementia. It sounded harsh, but Mrs Dunk was eighty-seven and she had been doing it for years. Her son was good about coming in once a month and paying up for her, though.

Selby just sat and stared. She tried not to slouch – she knew that was a bad look. So she sat as upright as possible, with a neutral expression on her face, and waited for a customer. It was a long wait. Selby had seen a TV documentary about meditation. She tried doing it now. She reasoned if she could let go of her physical self, this situation might not be so painfully boring. She focused on her breathing and emptying her mind. She started to feel heavy and relaxed.

Her head started to dip forward. She was just drifting off when . . .

'Do your homework!' snapped Mum.

Selby's head snapped up. She had a surge of adrenaline. Mum was glaring at her from the cooking section. Selby remembered she was in the bookstore, being punished. She shook herself to wake up more. She took out her folder from her bag and flipped to the maths section. It was quadratic equations. She didn't mind them. She had done all the homework at lunch. She wondered if she could get away with just sitting and staring at this page. No, that wasn't fair. Her mother was right. She should do her homework. Selby flipped to English.

The homework essay question stared back up at her. A wave of sadness washed over Selby. She really, really didn't want to write this essay. She closed her eyes, hoping it would go away. She flicked back to the maths. She would rather stare at that.

Just then, the shop bell tinkled. A customer. Selby's eyes flew open. A tall dark-skinned boy, a couple of years older than her, entered.

'Oh, it's you,' she said with a groan. It was just Dan, a friend of her brother's. All her brother's friends were annoying. They were all huge geeks who loved all the huge geek things. In her mind,

Dan would always be Sam Gamgee. He had dressed up as Sam to Eric's Frodo so they could go to their fourth-grade book parade as hobbits from *Lord of the Rings*. Dan was now six-foot-two and skinny, but he would always be a short hairy-footed creature to her.

'Exemplary customer service, little one,' said Dan.

'Whatever,' said Selby, picking up a pen and trying to focus on her work.

Dan walked over to the counter.

Selby ignored him. But he didn't go away. She glanced up. 'Can I help you?'

'I doubt it,' said Dan. 'I'm pretty sure I know the stock in this bookstore better than you do.'

Dan came to the bookstore every single day. When he was nine years old his mother had died. No-one knew what to do with him. His Dad was an electrician who had emigrated from Zimbabwe. He was a great dad, but he struggled to know what to say to his huge nerd son. Then Dan's grandfather had a good idea. He set up an account with the store and promised to buy Dan any book he wanted to read until he finished high school. Dan had, as a result, read a lot of books.

'Enjoy then,' said Selby, waving her arm at the store like a game show hostess waving at a new speed boat.

'I'm not here to have fun,' said Dan. 'I'm here to work.'

'Huh?' said Selby.

Dan smirked, 'They didn't tell you, did they?'

Selby got a horrible sinking feeling in her stomach. 'Tell me what?'

'I'm your new tutor,' said Dan. His smirk was positively a grin now. He was enjoying this too much. 'I hear you've been a very naughty girl. No homework for six months and throwing rocks at platypuses.'

'I didn't throw rocks at platypuses,' argued Selby.

Dan shook his head sadly. 'That's what all the juvenile delinquents say. Sadly, I can't cure you of your violent impulses. But I can help with the homework.'

'Urgh,' said Selby.

'Ah, Dan's here,' said Mum bustling down from the back of the store. 'So good to see you. Are you doing all right? Are you eating enough? You've grown so thin.'

'No, just taller, Mrs Michaels,' said Dan.

'So tall,' agreed Mum. 'It's just not right. You boys grow up so fast. Here, eat something.'

17

There was a candy jar on the counter. Kids were given a piece when they bought a book. It was also handy for when kids threw tantrums in the store if their parents spent too long browsing. Mum grabbed a handful of mini chocolate bars and stuffed them in Dan's jacket pocket.

'Is your dad feeding you enough?' she asked. 'I can always send over a home-cooked meal.'

Selby snorted back a laugh. Mum was not a good cook. Mum glared at Selby. 'I hope you're ready to work,' she said.

'I thought you were going to get me a proper tutor,' said Selby.

'Dan is a proper tutor,' said Mrs Michaels. 'We were lucky to get him. He's the top tutor in town.'

'I could have ridden my bike over the bridge,' said Selby. The next town over was the other side of the river. They had a coaching clinic there, staffed by people who had not gone to the same high school as her.

'And who knows what mischief you would have got up to,' accused Mum, 'when you stopped to throw rocks along the way.'

Selby rolled her eyes. She was branded. That was

the thing about living in a country town – once word got out that you'd done something strange, it would stay with you for the rest of your life. She'd be in her nineties and people would still point at her and say she was the one who threw rocks at wildlife. Truth and reality didn't matter.

'Let's go upstairs,' said Selby.

'No, you're staying where I can see you,' snapped Mum.

'You want me to work right here in the shop?' asked Selby.

'I think you can handle the workload,' said her mother sarcastically, before stomping off to the back of the store again. Selby wondered how long it would be before Mum forgot to be mad at her. It looked like this was going to last for weeks. Or at least until Mum found a good book to read and tuned her out again.

'Shall we get started?' asked Dan.

Selby couldn't believe this was actually going to happen. She was going to be tutored by her brother's geeky friend. She felt bad about upsetting her parents and letting them down, but this was the first moment that she felt sorry for herself and genuinely

19

wished she hadn't stopped doing all her homework six months ago.

It was one thing to be a woefully ignorant embarrassment to your family. But to do it in full view of a smirking eighteen-year-old, who was going to repeat anything you said to your insufferable older brother, was a nightmare.

'Why are you even here?' asked Selby.

'Because your parents are paying me by the hour,' said Dan.

'No, I mean, why are you still here in town?' asked Selby. 'Everyone else went off to uni. I'm sure you must have been smart enough to get into some course in advanced nerd studies or something.'

'I did,' said Dan. 'I'm deferring for a year or two. I promised I'd stay and help Dad.'

'Oh,' said Selby. That didn't sound like fun.

'I'll probably learn more here anyway,' said Dan.

'How do you figure that?' asked Selby.

'Anywhere there are people there will be endless intrigue to observe,' said Dan.

'Really?' said Selby.

'Sure,' said Dan. 'Jane Austen barely went anywhere but she found seven books' worth of stories to tell. Look at you. You're a prime example. By all appearances you're a small-town delinquent, but I'm sure even you have hidden depths.'

Selby just grunted. She may not have read any Jane Austen books but she had seen plenty of TV adaptations. She knew Jane Austen didn't exactly explore a vast variety of themes – all her books were romance novels about young women. But Selby had learned many years ago that there was no point arguing with her brother or his friends. They could always out-talk her. It didn't seem fair. It didn't make them right just because they sounded right.

'Besides,' said Dan. 'I can learn anything and travel anywhere without leaving town. That is the magic of books. I can travel around the world, into space, back and forth in time. I can walk in a woman's shoes in seventeenth century Paris or sit at the trial of Socrates in ancient Greece. All through the power of reading.'

Selby rolled her eyes and sighed. She was used to this sort of crazy idealistic talk from her parents. 'Whatever,' she said.

'So, shall we start?' asked Dan.

'Sure,' said Selby. She might have a complex mass

of feelings on the subject, but that didn't mean she intended to share them.

Dan came around behind the counter and sat on the stool next to her so he could look over her shoulder.

'Is that your maths homework?' he asked.

'Ahuh,' said Selby.

'You've done it already,' said Dan.

Selby didn't respond except to roll her eyes at him.

'Why don't we start on something you haven't done yet?' suggested Dan.

Selby flicked through the pages of her folder. The biology section was at the back. She liked biology. It was her favourite subject. She didn't particularly enjoy it, but she didn't hate it as much as everything else. And Mrs Denison let her take her shoes off in class, which she appreciated.

Dan's hand flew out and blocked her flicking. 'Let's stop here, in English,' said Dan.

Selby's shoulders slumped.

'I hear you're struggling with that,' said Dan.

A lump formed in Selby's throat. Oh my gosh, she did not want to cry in front of this boy. Not about something as dumb as her English marks.

Dan flicked through to the most recent notes. 'Is this your new assignment?' He pointed to a page that had just one sentence written at the top. It was an essay question.

What is Hamlet's beef? Discuss.

'Beef?' said Dan.

'You know, it's slang, for when you've got a problem with someone,' said Selby.

'I know what "beef" means,' said Dan, 'I just can't believe it's in an essay question. Let me guess, you've got Ms Karim for English?'

Selby nodded.

'She always wants to make things relatable to teens,' said Dan. 'It's ridiculous. The point of literature is that it should already be relatable to everyone. Dumbing it down with colloquialisms just discourages young people from developing a full vocabulary.'

Selby had stopped listening. She was doodling on the margin of the page.

'So, what's your opinion?' asked Dan. 'What is Hamlet's beef, dude?'

'I don't know,' said Selby.

'Well, what was he complaining about in the play?' asked Dan.

Selby shrugged.

'I know you can speak your mind,' said Dan. 'I heard you screaming at Eric when he used your favourite t-shirt to mop up a coke spill.'

'I haven't read the play,' Selby snapped out.

Dan threw up his hands. 'Why not?' He flipped back through her notes. 'You've been studying this for . . . three weeks already!'

Selby looked about for any opportunity of escape. Perhaps her mother was spontaneously combusting in the back of the store.

'Where's your copy of the play?' asked Dan.

'I don't know,' said Selby.

'How can you not know?' asked Dan. He was actually getting angry, like he was a real teacher or something.

'I lent my copy to Bree,' said Selby. 'She left hers in her pocket and it went through the washing machine.'

'So you had no intention of reading it?' asked Dan.

'I haven't read any of the school's set texts for two years,' said Selby. 'I didn't think the teachers would notice. They never have before.'

Dan took a deep breath. 'I've never had to tutor someone with quite your attitude before,' he said.

'I didn't want a tutor,' said Selby.

'You prefer failure?' asked Dan.

'I prefer not having a tutor,' said Selby.

'Well, this is a bookstore,' said Dan. 'Go and fetch a copy. We'll read it together.'

Selby actually groaned.

'I can understand not liking a subject like PE, because that can be physically painful,' said Dan. 'But this is just reading. It doesn't hurt.'

'For me, it does,' grumbled Selby.

She slid off her stool and wound her way to the darkest, least-frequented section of the store where they kept the classics. She found a copy of *Hamlet*. There were a lot in stock because the kids at the high school always studied it in year 11. Selby laid the brand new copy down on the counter.

Dan opened it up and flicked past the introduction. 'Here we go . . . act one, scene one.' He slid the book across so it was in front of Selby. 'Read,' he instructed.

Selby laid her hand on the book to hold the page open. It was so new, the pristine spine was trying to force the pages shut. She bent her head over the text and tried to read.

AOTCEN SOCENENE.

The letters swam in front of her eyes. But she had to do this. She concentrated and the words started to emerge . . .

ACTONE SCENEONE.

'Out loud,' said Dan.

'Huh?' Selby looked up.

'Read it out loud,' said Dan.

'You're kidding?' said Selby.

'No, it's a play,' said Dan. 'It's meant to be heard aloud. Not read in your head.'

Selby blushed, 'I'm not reading aloud. Not here, in the store.'

'Why not?' asked Dan. 'It's a bookstore. An empty bookstore. It's the perfect place to read a good book.'

'I read slow,' mumbled Selby

'Slowly,' corrected Dan. 'You need the "ly" on

the end. And it doesn't matter if you read slowly. I'm being paid by the hour. It's better for me if you take longer.' He grinned.

Selby's heart sank. She wasn't really too slow at reading, but it took her longer than other people because her brain danced about as she read. It was like every line was a word scramble. Her brain noticed every possible word permutation before going back and working out the most likely phrase. But then sometimes her brain went off on tangents, thinking about the other letter combinations, especially if they were more interesting. Before she knew it, half an hour had gone by and she had only read one page and had no idea what had happened in the plot. So she could read. It just took a lot of focus.

Selby looked at the words. She needed to concentrate. She was determined not to embarrass herself in front of her brother's nerd friend. Sometimes it helped if she ran a finger under the words as she read. She knew it looked babyish, but she'd rather that than stuff up now. Selby pointed to the first word, focused in on the shape of each letter and started to read aloud . . .

BARNARDO	*Who's there?*
FRANCISCO	*Nay, answer me. Stand and unfold yourself!*

She stopped. 'Well, what does that mean?' asked Selby. '"Nay" – that's what horses say. And "unfold yourself". It sounds like he's talking to a stack of ironing.'

'Don't overthink it,' said Dan. 'Just let the words wash over you. It's always confusing when you first start hearing Shakespeare, but then your brain adjusts and you start to understand it all from the context.'

'It'd take more than a brain adjustment,' muttered Selby.

'Just read,' said Dan.

Selby took a deep breath and started reading the dialogue again . . .

BARNARDO	*Long live the king!*
FRANCISCO	*Barnardo?*
BARNARDO	*He.*
FRANCISCO	*You come most carefully upon your hour.*

BARNARDO   *'Tis now struck twelve. Get thee*
           to bed, Francisco.
FRANCISCO *For this relief much thanks.*
           'Tis bitter cold,
           And I am sick at heart.

Tinkle, tinkle, tinkle.

Selby's head snapped up. It was the shop's bell. A customer had entered. 'Cookbooks?' the customer asked.

'Down the back,' said Selby. 'Mum's organising stock there. She'll be able to help you.'

Selby glanced at Dan. He was staring at her. It made her self-conscious. 'What?' she asked.

'You have a beautiful voice,' said Dan. 'You read very well.'

Selby looked into his eyes. She didn't often make eye contact with anyone, but she couldn't believe he was serious. His big brown eyes were like wells into his soul. He wasn't lying. Suddenly she wished he was. She looked away.

'No, I don't,' said Selby. He had to be making fun of her. 'That's ridiculous.'

'You do,' said Dan. 'It's melodic. Almost magical. Keep reading.'

Selby focused in again.

BARNARDO	*Have you had quiet guard?*
FRANCISCO	*Not a mouse stirring.*
BARNARDO	*Well, good night.*
	If you do meet Horatio and Marcellus,
	The rivals of my watch, bid them make haste.

Selby was beginning to enjoy saying the words. The serifs of the letters felt like tails on her tongue. Every curl was a swoop and a wave into the energy of the story. She could practically smell the ink. She could almost hear the scratch of the quill as she imagined Shakespeare scrawling each word on the page. She felt warm, but in a good way – so comfortable, so right. The blood was rushing in her ears, but she could still hear her own voice.

FRANCISCO	*Stand ho! Who is there?*
HORATIO	*Friends to this ground.*

MARCELLUS   *And liegemen to the Dane.*
FRANCISCO   *Give you good night.*

Gradually Selby felt herself being drawn down, like the pull of gravity, through the page, into the book then into the ether. There was a tremendous rushing of wind and words. She wasn't in the bookstore anymore. She was travelling, but not through space or even time. She could still hear her own voice, punctuated by the mumble and applause of a crowd.

HORATIO   *But look, the morn in russet*
            mantle clad
            Walks o'er the dew of yon high
            eastward hill.
            Break we our watch up, and
            by my advice
            Let us impart what we have seen
            tonight
            Unto young Hamlet; for upon
            my life
            This spirit, dumb to us, will speak
            to him.

And then . . .

WHACK!

Selby was lying flat on her back on a cold stone floor. It was a freezing, black night. She was staring straight up at the sky. There were no stars, but she could make out clouds whipping across with the wind, giving the occasional glimpse of the moon.

'Where am I?' she whispered.

A hand grasped hers. Selby flinched, but when she turned, it was Dan. He was collapsed on the ground a short distance from her.

'Selby?' he said. There was panic in his eyes. 'Where are we?'

3

Another World

Selby looked about. She could barely see anything in the dark, but everything was wrong. It was cold. It was damp. It was night-time.

'I don't know,' said Selby. They appeared to be on top of a stone fortification, like an old castle. Over the sound of the wind, she could make out waves crashing in the distance. 'I can hear the sea.'

'It's freezing,' said Dan. He was only wearing a t-shirt and denim jacket. That was nothing to this biting cold.

The wind was making her eyes water. There was so little light. How could she be sitting on top of a stone wall? There were no stone buildings in town. And what little she could see looked like battlements.

33

There was a long narrow walkway and a wall lined with turrets. Like something out of a Robin Hood movie. A wall built for archers or cannons to fire between the stonework.

Selby was starting to feel very frightened. This was wrong. Very wrong. 'We've got to get back,' said Selby.

'But what happened?' asked Dan. 'How did we get here? How *do* we go back?'

Selby sat up and started to feel about with her hands. She was trying to find a door or a passageway, perhaps something that they had somehow fallen through.

She was already frightened and panicked, but as she crouched on the ground a growing sense of horrible dread washed over her. It had nothing to do with the strange situation she found herself in. It was a visceral response to something wrong. She had never been so afraid.

Selby tried to calm herself. There was nothing to fear. It was just darkness and cold. And yet Selby felt a looming sense of doom like nothing she'd ever known before. Cold, horrible feelings washed over her. Adrenalin started to surge in her veins.

Selby wanted to run. But where to in this strange place and complete darkness? She was already cold but now she was so viscerally terrified she felt like she had pins and needles. She finally understood what the expression to have your 'hair stand on end' felt like.

'What's happening?' she asked Dan.

'I don't know,' said Dan, his voice quavering. He couldn't hide his fear. 'You feel it too?'

Then Selby saw it. 'Look!' she said in a terrified whisper. There was something coming towards them, from behind Dan. Something glowing. A light. But normally light is comforting in the dark when you're afraid. This pale shimmering shape was ominous.

'What is it?' asked Dan.

The shape was coming towards them, growing larger. 'It looks like a man,' said Selby, squinting into the roiling black night, trying to see in spite of the wind in her eyes.

The sense of dread grew stronger as the light approached.

'We should get out of here,' said Dan.

He pulled Selby back with him, but they didn't manage to scramble far in the darkness before they found themselves backed into a corner in the battlements.

Selby was so frightened now she could barely move. They could see the shape more clearly. It was a man, an older man, wearing military armour and he was lumbering towards them at a steady, resigned pace. He must have been able to see them, but he did not seem interested. He looked straight through them.

As he drew closer, they could see it was not really a man. They could see right through him. He was only shimmering light in the form of a man.

Selby knew what she was looking at. 'It's a ghost,' she whispered.

Dan wrapped his arm around Selby and pulled her in close to the corner with him so they were crouched down tight up against the wall. They held their breaths and waited to see how the ghost would respond to them. But it never looked down, even though it passed by less than a metre away.

As the ghost moved further away, the feeling of dread eased. Selby gulped in a huge calming breath. She shakily pushed off Dan's arm and got to her feet, watching the ghost disappear in the dark distance.

'I know where we are,' said Dan. He was still crouched in the corner. He appeared to be in shock.

Selby could barely hear him over the wind, 'What?'

'Look out!' said Dan.

There was the sound of running footsteps, but Selby had no time to turn before something big slammed into her. She was knocked off her feet and crashed into the ground. Her first thought was she had been attacked by a wild animal, but she soon realised it was a man.

The man was much bigger than her, which wasn't saying much. Selby was hardly tall. She had been winded by the fall. Now she couldn't move under his weight. He was panting heavily. He pushed himself up and in the dim light she got a glimpse of his face. He was young – perhaps only a couple of years older than Dan – and he was good-looking. Although all Selby really noticed was his eyes. He had piercing blue eyes. Selby found herself staring into them as he stared back. This young man looked haunted and grief-stricken.

'Are you okay?' asked Selby.

'What are you?' the young man choked out in a hoarse voice. He sounded frightened too. 'Some sort of temporal being, sent by the devil to haunt my waking hours? Or an angel, sent to guide me in my troubles?'

'I'm Selby,' said Selby. She would have liked to have gotten up. It was embarrassing to be having a conversation when you were pressed against the ground. 'I'm no-one special.'

'Nay, I'll not believe that,' said the young man.

'MURDER!'

A horrible, sonorous voice bellowed out from behind them. The sound echoed off the stonework and whipped about them on the wind. The young man sprang to his feet and took off in the direction of the cry. Selby scrambled up. She watched him run over to the ghost. He slowed as he drew near and knelt in front of it.

Selby started to follow. Dan grabbed her arm. 'Where are you going?' he asked.

'He might need help,' said Selby.

Dan went with her as she drew closer.

The ghost spoke again in a slow ponderous voice. 'If thou didst ever thy dear father love . . .'

'Oh God!' whimpered the young man.

'. . . . Revenge his foul and most unnatural murder,' ordered the ghost.

'Murder?' said the young man. He seemed astonished and frightened.

'Murder most foul,' said the ghost.

'What's going on?' asked Selby.

'Shhh,' said Dan. 'Listen.'

'Sleeping within my orchard,' explained the ghost. 'My custom always of the afternoon. Upon my secure hour thy uncle stole. With juice of cursed hebenon in a vial. And in the porches of my ears did pour the leperous distilment.'

Selby could not believe what she was overhearing. 'Did he just say that he died because someone poured poison in his ear?' asked Selby. 'Would that even work? I've watched a lot of CSI and crime shows. That does not sound plausible.'

'Shhh,' said Dan, pointing at the ghost, encouraging her to keep listening to that conversation.

'Mine uncle?' asked the young man.

'Ay, that incestuous, that adulterate beast,' accused the ghost. 'Oh Hamlet, what a falling off was there . . .'

'Hamlet?!' exclaimed Selby. Luckily the wind was so loud and Hamlet was far enough away he didn't overhear. Or did overhear and was too consumed by the presence of his father's ghost. Selby turned to Dan in shock. 'That's Hamlet? *The* Hamlet? The Prince of Denmark?'

'We must be inside the play,' whispered Dan.

'How can we be inside a play?' asked Selby.

'I don't know,' said Dan. 'But we are. There's Hamlet and his father, the ghost. This is the castle of the Danish king. We're standing on the battlements of Castle Elsinore! It's all so real.'

There was no denying it – the stonework, the wind, the biting cold and the horror of the ghost. These weren't things of dreams. These couldn't be imagined. They could only be experienced. And what Selby was experiencing didn't just feel real. It was real.

They turned back to listen to the conversation again. The ghost was describing his own murder. 'In an instant, sores formed about my smooth body with vile and loathsome crust,' spoke the ghost. 'Thus was I, sleeping, by a brother's hand – of life, of crown, of queen at once dispatched.'

'Oh villain, villain, smiling, damned villain!' exclaimed Hamlet. He clutched at his own ears as if to block the terrible truth, too horrified to hear the details of his father's death.

The ghost was looking out to the horizon. The soft red glow of daybreak was beginning to form. 'The glow worm shows the morning to be near. Adieu, adieu, adieu. Remember me.' The ghost disappeared fading into the night.

'Remember thee?' said Hamlet. 'Ay, thou poor ghost, while memory holds a seat in this distracted globe. I'll remember thee.'

'This is crazy,' Selby whispered to Dan.

'Yes,' said Dan. 'That's pretty much the theme of the play.'

'Did you just go into tutor mode?' asked Selby.

'I told you if you saw the play performed live it would make more sense to you,' said Dan.

Hamlet was walking back towards them. As he drew close, Selby could see that he was shaking with agitation and fear. He was probably having the world's biggest adrenalin rush too.

'Thou art still here?' said Hamlet. He seemed awed by Selby. He reached out and touched her on the side of her face as if testing that she was real.

'I feared you were an apparition too,' said Hamlet. 'I hoped an angel.'

'I'm just a normal girl,' said Selby.

'I pray 'tis true,' said Hamlet. He grasped her hand, holding her fingers in his. 'Thou art so fair. Art thou a nymph? If so, remember me in your prayers. I shall need the prayers of all good souls.'

'Okay,' said Selby. She didn't really understand him, and she was wildly uncomfortable that someone so good-looking was holding her hand and staring into her eyes, but it seemed easiest just to agree.

Suddenly, Hamlet's attitude changed. Like he was snapping back into business mode. 'Yea, from the table of my memory I'll wipe away all trivial fond records.' He took a step away from Selby and turned back to where he had seen his father's ghost, as if to talk to him again. 'And thy commandment all alone shall live within the book and volume of my brain, unmixed with baser matter – yea, by heaven!'

'I'm not following this,' Selby whispered to Dan.

'He's giving himself a talking to,' Dan explained quietly. 'Hamlet does this a lot throughout the play. He's saying he's got to forget about everything else and focus on avenging his father's death.'

'Right,' said Selby. 'It doesn't sound like a healthy father-son relationship. I'm pretty sure my dad would not expect Eric to kill our uncle if he thought he had been murdered.'

'Isn't your uncle a hedge-fund analyst in Singapore?' asked Dan.

'Yeah, not really the murderous type,' said Selby.

Hamlet turned back to them. He clasped her by the shoulder. Selby winced. Hamlet had really strong hands and he was gripping her tightly.

'You must swear to me,' urged Hamlet, 'that you will say nothing of what you have seen here tonight.'

'Don't worry,' said Selby. 'No-one would believe me if I tried.'

'Swear it,' ordered Hamlet, shaking her slightly by the shoulder. The fear was wearing off and his eyes were starting to burn with intensity. Selby didn't really like the way he was giving her an order.

'Okay,' said Selby. 'I swear.'

Hamlet seemed to sense her reluctance. He suddenly drew his sword. 'Swear on my sword!' he demanded.

Selby bristled. She was generally a very easy-going person, but deep down she was a feminist, and she did not like being given an order by a man. Especially not one who was, however unconsciously, being physically intimidating. The worst part about the order was his clear expectation that she would follow it.

'You didn't say the magic word,' said Selby.

'Selby, just do as he says,' urged Dan.

Hamlet noticed Dan for the first time. It was really dark and Dan did have dark skin. He was easy to miss in the shadows.

'Who's this?' demanded Hamlet, turning his sword and pointing it at Dan's throat.

'Hey,' protested Selby. 'Don't do that. He's a friend.'

'How can I be sure?' asked Hamlet.

'You can't,' said Selby, grabbing hold of Dan and pulling him behind her. 'But you can't kill everyone you meet on the off chance you won't get along with them later.'

'You are from a distant land,' said Hamlet, eyeing Dan.

'I am Selby's servant,' said Dan.

'What?' said Selby.

Dan kicked the side of her foot and raised his eyebrows. He clearly wanted her to go along with this. But Selby wasn't going to go along with pretending that Dan was a servant just because he was of African heritage.

'Dan is my tutor,' said Selby. 'A wise man and an educator.'

'So you are fellow student,' said Hamlet. This seemed to please him. He lowered his sword. 'I am on leave from the university at Wittenberg. I came home to bury my father.' He turned to glance back at the spot where he had been talking to his father's ghost.

'I'm sorry for your loss,' said Selby.

'It is an honest ghost, that, let me tell you,' said Hamlet. But from the beseeching look in his eye, he seemed to be convincing himself more than her. Hamlet held out his sword again, but in a less threatening gesture. This time, even though he did not say please, he at least sounded like he was asking, not ordering. 'Swear you will not say a word of what you have seen here. Mine uncle must not know of this.'

'SWEAR!' The ghost's voice suddenly bellowed out. The stonework shook with the unnatural force. Selby, Dan and Hamlet were physically shaken, hit by the shock wave of sound.

'Do as it says,' pleaded Hamlet. A hysterical smile was coming to his face. 'Swear it.'

Selby could see that this was all too much for the young prince. He was not coping. He looked like he could cry or laugh, or do both simultaneously. She reached out and covered his hand on the hilt of the sword. 'I swear,' she said.

Hamlet looked at Dan. 'Swear it.'

Dan reached out too. 'I swear,' he said.

The rumbling from the ghost's cry drew silent. The only sound was the wind.

'There are stranger things in heaven and earth than in our imaginations, Selby,' muttered Hamlet.

'I know,' Selby said kindly. 'Come on, let's get you inside out of the cold. This is a lot to take in. You're probably going to go into shock. And if *you* don't, I will.'

'Ay,' said Hamlet. 'The time is out of joint. Oh cursed spite, that ever I was born to set it right.'

Hamlet started heading back along the battlements towards the staircase that lead down to the castle. Dan and Selby followed behind him. But as they reached the spot where they had first arrived, Selby grabbed Dan's jacket sleeve.

'This is it,' said Selby.

'What?' said Dan.

'The spot where we arrived,' said Selby, she dropped to her hands and knees and started feeling the floor. 'There must be some sort of porthole that we came through. We need to find it and get back to the bookstore.'

'Are you kidding?' protested Dan.

Selby looked up.

'We can't go back,' said Dan. 'We're in *Hamlet*.'

4

Crossroads

'We've got to get back,' whispered Selby. 'I don't want to stay trapped in a time when antibiotics, electric lighting and television haven't been invented yet.'

'What is it with you and television?' asked Dan.

'Nothing like this ever happened to me from watching television,' said Selby.

'Don't blame the play,' said Dan.

'Fine, I'll blame you,' said Selby. 'You made me read the play.'

'But this is amazing,' said Dan. 'We're here with Hamlet! We're on top of the castle in Elsinore with the Prince of Denmark.'

'Now is not the time to nerd out on me,' said

Selby, shaking his arm as though she was trying to wake him from a dream.

'This is amazing. We're in a world created by Shakespeare,' marvelled Dan.

'That's not even possible,' said Selby. 'I refuse to believe it. I must be having a brain haemorrhage or a stroke. That's the only logical explanation.'

'Am I having a stroke too?' asked Dan. 'Because I'm experiencing the exact same visual and auditory delusion.'

'No, you don't exist either,' said Selby. 'You're just another one of my stroke symptoms.'

Dan pinched her on the arm.

'Ow!' said Selby. 'What was that for?'

'Do stroke symptoms pinch?' asked Dan.

'I don't know,' said Selby. 'I've never had a stroke before.' She stomped hard on his foot.

'Ow!' cried Dan, clutching his foot and hopping on the other one. 'What was that for.'

'The fun of it,' said Selby. 'Come on, let's go back.'

'Where?' asked Dan.

'To the bookstore,' said Selby.

'Are you kidding?!' said Dan. 'This is mind-blowing. We're inside Shakespeare's greatest creation!'

'This is wrong,' said Selby. 'It defies the laws of physics, the space-time continuum and common sense. We need to get back to reality.'

'Reality is overrated,' said Dan. 'We're in a work of art. We should explore.'

'But what about home?' said Selby.

'Home will always be there,' said Dan. 'We're here now. This is an amazing opportunity.'

'What ho, Selby!' called Hamlet from the top of the staircase. 'Where art thou?'

'Coming, my lord,' called Dan.

'My lord?' said Selby.

'He's a prince,' said Dan. 'You're supposed to call him "my lord".'

'La-di-dah,' said Selby.

'Come on,' said Dan, grabbing her hand and pulling her towards the staircase. 'It'll be fun. You might even learn something.'

'What?' asked Selby, pulling away from him. 'Why does everybody obsess about fiction and what fiction means? Like reality isn't enough to deal with?'

'Shakespeare had more insight into humanity and empathy than anyone,' said Dan. 'And he had a magical command of the English language, so he could perfectly convey ideas that had never been expressed before. And here we are – you and me – two small-town kids, inside his imagination! It's unbelievable. We can't just leave.'

'Yeah, we totally can,' said Selby. 'This is insane. We can't get trapped here.'

'Why not?' asked Dan.

'Because you can't run away to the circus,' said Selby, 'if the circus is four hundred years old and fictional!'

'No, I'm not running away,' said Dan. He waved his hands in frustration as he tried to explain to her. 'This is the literary equivalent of discovering the North Pole. Or travelling to the moon. It's epic. We can't leave.'

'What if we're trapped here?' asked Selby.

'It's worth the risk,' said Dan.

'Are you out of your mind?' asked Selby. 'I am sixteen years old. I have my whole life ahead of me. I do not want to get trapped in a play set in sixteenth-century Denmark. Apart from it being crazy-ass cold here and everyone talking in incomprehensible archaic English, I'm pretty sure the flush toilet has not been invented yet.'

'So you just want to go back to your boring small-town life?' asked Dan.

'Yes!' cried Selby. 'I like being bored. I'm comfortable with bored. It's what I'm used to.'

'Well, I want more,' said Dan. 'It's okay for you. You'll finish school and go off to the city. Not me. I'm stuck in our town. I can't go to uni. I can't travel.'

'What are you talking about?' asked Selby.

'Dad has liver disease,' said Dan. 'He's not getting better.'

'Oh, Dan,' sighed Selby.

'This may be my only chance to explore,' he was pleading now.

'But what if you get stuck here?' said Selby.

'I'd rather be stuck here than at home,' said Dan. He wasn't looking at her anymore. He was watching Hamlet disappear down a staircase into the castle. Selby could tell Dan wanted to hurry after him.

'What about all that stuff about being able to travel anywhere through the magic of books?' asked Selby.

Dan glanced back and smiled wryly, 'It came true, didn't it? Literally. Here we are.'

'Eugh,' said Selby. She realised he was exactly right while also being a total hypocrite.

'Come on,' said Dan. 'We should follow him.'

'This is crazy,' said Selby.

Dan was barely listening, 'The night watch will be along soon, and it'll be harder to explain to them why a black man and a teenage girl wearing trousers are up here in the middle of the night.' Dan hurried off.

'Dan!' Selby called after him. She was so afraid. Suddenly she longed for the bookstore. She might not like books, and she might be arguing with Mum and Dad, but everything about the bookstore – the smell, the warmth, the familiarity – it all represented safety. She wanted to get back there.

Selby crouched down and felt about on the stonework, trying to find where they had come in. The stones were cold and wet. She couldn't be sure she was even in the right spot, it was so dark. But then she touched it. One stone that felt different. It was warm. Selby leaned in and pushed gently on this one stone. Beneath her hand, it began to vibrate. She could hear a noise. It sounded like muttering. She pressed harder and it was like she was turning up the volume on the radio, only what she could hear was her own voice – reading *Hamlet*.

HAMLET   *And what so poor a man as*
         Hamlet is
         May do t'express his love and
         friending to you,
         God willing, shall not lack. Let us
         go in together . . .

Selby pushed harder into the stone. The whisper grew louder and her hand started to move through the wall.

HAMLET   *And still your fingers on your lips,*
         I pray.
         The time is out of joint. O cursèd
         spite,
         That ever I was born to set it right.
         Nay come, let's go together.

'Selby, come on!'

Selby snapped back to reality. Well, this Shakespearean reality. Dan was calling to her from over by

54

the staircase. Selby could only see him in silhouette against the dim light coming from inside.

Her hand felt warm against the stone. The warmth and comfort of the bookstore was just on the other side. She could be back there in a moment. She imagined Mum and Dad, still angry with her, but somehow that was comforting too.

'Selby!' called Dan.

Selby imagined Dan's dad. She imagined the look on his face when he came to the store looking for Dan, and she couldn't explain where he was. That look would be heartbreaking. She couldn't do that. She had to take Dan back to him.

Selby sighed. She pulled her hand back into the cold of the Danish night, got to her feet and hurried after Dan. The play was only four hours long. She could hang on that long to make sure Dan got back.

5

Love

Selby hurried down the spiral staircase. It was disconcerting, going round and round. The steps were not quite even, so she had to concentrate not to lose her footing. She began to feel dizzy and disorientated. The stone wall was damp with condensation, but she kept her palm against it as she jogged down the steps, not wanting to fall.

Suddenly the staircase opened out. Now it was bright daylight. They had been through another transformation – a wormhole in the narrative. They weren't inside the castle anymore. They seemed to be inside a house. Dan was already standing there, marvelling at everything in the room.

'Where are we?' asked Selby. 'When are we? How come it's daylight?'

'It's a play,' said Dan. 'There's been a scene change. This must be act one, scene three.'

'Huh?' said Selby.

'Polonius's house,' explained Dan. 'He's the king's advisor. His son Laertes is about to leave, and Polonius will be giving him worldly advice before he goes off on his travels. It's some of the most famous and most frequently quoted bits in all of Shakespeare. You've got to see it. This stuff will definitely come up in class discussions at school.'

Together, they crept through the house. They could hear voices up ahead – an old man talking to a young man, perhaps in his early twenties. The old man was very well dressed but from his manner he seemed pompous and silly. The young man seemed to be taking some effort to keep a straight face.

'. . . Give every man thy ear, but few thy voice,' said the older man. 'Take each man's censure, but reserve thy judgement . . .'

'That's Polonius talking,' whispered Dan. He hurried along the corridor and listened at the doorway.

'. . . Neither a borrower or a lender be, for loan oft loses both itself and friend,' advised Polonius. 'And this above all, to thine own self be true.'

'I've heard that one,' said Selby.

'Shakespeare came up with all these sayings,' said Dan. 'You're watching the birth of so many common expressions.'

Selby peeked around the doorway so she could get a glimpse of Polonius and Laertes. She was confused. These were supposed to be wise words, but they seemed silly coming from Polonius – someone who might be smartly dressed and have an impressive amount of facial hair, but who was clearly a fool.

'Wow!' gasped Dan.

'What?' said Selby.

She turned to see what Dan was looking at. There was a girl coming down the stairs into the corridor where they were standing. She was utterly stunning. Selby had seen plenty of pretty people before – even a couple of beautiful people – but not this level of beauty. It was other-worldly. Her hair was neither blonde nor brown, it was more of a golden colour somewhere in between. It shone. Her face was pale but soft and angelic. She looked like she was smiling even when she wasn't smiling. Her posture and her clothes were all perfect and elegant. Everything about her was the ideal of virtuous femininity. Just looking at her made Selby feel small. She never even looked neat. Not even when she was trying to. She had a scruffy soul, and that always came through.

Selby turned to Dan to ask a question, but from the look on his face – it was as if he had been stunned. Like a deer in the headlights of a truck about to hit it. His mouth literally hung open, a stupid dazed look in his eyes, as he watched the girl descend.

'Who is it?' asked Selby.

'Ophelia,' whispered Dan.

'Oh,' said Selby. Even she had heard of Ophelia. She was an icon among literary characters. Selby didn't know a lot about the play. But she knew Ophelia was Hamlet's girlfriend. And that she drowned. Or she would drown. Although at the moment, she was very much alive and glowing with beauty.

Dan unconsciously stepped forward. His feet were drawn to her.

Ophelia noticed him. 'Pardon me, sir,' said Ophelia. 'I did not see you there.'

'I saw you,' said Dan.

Ophelia blushed and glanced down shyly.

Selby rolled her eyes. 'Come on, we've got to go,' urged Selby, before nodding to Ophelia. 'Nice to meet you.' Grabbing Dan by the arm, Selby pulled him out of the house. Once they were in the brisk air of the courtyard, Dan seemed to gather himself.

'What was that about?' asked Selby.

'What?' said Dan.

'Does your tongue taste of carpet?' asked Selby. 'Because that's how far it was hanging out of your head.'

'She was stunning,' said Dan.

'Yes, I know,' said Selby. 'But surely you can retain some use of your intellect when you see a pretty girl.'

'She wasn't pretty,' said Dan. 'She was beautiful. Stunning.'

'Yes, you've used that word already, thesaurus boy,' said Selby. 'Nice to know that hormones are such a handbrake on your intellect. Come on, you've had a look around. You've met a pretty girl. Can we go home now?'

'To the bookstore?' asked Dan. He was still dazed.

'Yes!' said Selby. 'Home. You remember home.' She was getting upset. It was one thing to be stuck in medieval Denmark, but she definitely didn't want to be stuck with someone who was brain addled with lust.

Dan relented slightly. 'Soon,' he said. 'There's a good bit coming up. The actors will arrive for the play within the play. That's crucial to the whole plot. You'll probably get an essay question on it in your exam.'

'I don't care about my exam!' said Selby.

'We're here now,' said Dan. 'Please. Let's just stay for that bit. It's really good, I promise. Come on, we need to find the main gates of the castle. That's where the players arrive.' Dan hurried to a passageway between two buildings. Selby didn't have much choice. She followed him in. The passageway was very dark. When they emerged, it was not into another courtyard – they were in the royal throne room.

Selby spun round, there was no passageway behind her.

'Did we just go through another wormhole?' asked Selby.

'We're in another scene,' Dan whispered. 'Act two, scene two.'

'What does that mean?' asked Selby.

'That we are in the presence of . . .' said Dan, pointing to an elegantly dressed, middle-aged couple sitting at the far end of the room, '. . . the King and Queen of Denmark.'

The king and queen were the focus of the whole room, like they had been arranged for a perfectly composed portrait. They were flanked by courtiers and servants, but their thrones were raised so they sat above everybody else. They radiated consequence. As Selby watched, the king reached across and took his wife's hand. The queen smiled at him.

'They're newlyweds,' said Dan.

Selby realised that made sense. They did look like a loving couple. It was unusual to see an older couple take such simple pleasure in a small gesture of affection.

'But then, isn't that Hamlet's uncle? The guy who killed the ghost?' whispered Selby. They were a good thirty metres away from anyone else and there was no chance they could be overheard.

'Yes,' said Dan. 'At least that's the ghost's version of events.'

'He doesn't look like a murderer,' said Selby. The

king was immaculately dressed in fine robes befitting his station. But more than that, he looked personally composed and authoritative.

'What do murderers look like?' asked Dan.

'Not that regal,' said Selby. 'They're meant to have unwashed hair, dirty clothes and drive panel vans.'

The door near Selby and Dan pushed open. A courtier led in two young men.

The king called out to them, 'Welcome, dear Rosencrantz and Guildenstern!'

'It's them!' said Dan under his breath. 'They're Hamlet's childhood friends. The king has sent for them because he wants them to spy on Hamlet.'

'Classic manipulative-parent move,' said Selby.

'He makes out it's because he's concerned for Hamlet's mental health,' said Dan. 'Listen . . .'

The king and queen were talking to Rosencrantz and Guildenstern. The young men seemed over-awed to be in conversation with the royal couple.

'The need we have to use you did provoke our hasty sending,' said the king as the young men approached him. 'I entreat you both that, being of so young days brought up with him – that you draw him on to pleasures – to gather so much as you may glean. Whether something unknown to us afflicts him, that lies within our remedy.'

'Good gentlemen,' added the queen. 'Hamlet hath much talked of you. And sure I am two men there are not living to whom he more adheres. If it will please you to expend your time with us awhile for the supply and profit of our hope.'

Selby whispered to Dan, 'And the friends just go along with this?'

'Ahuh,' said Dan. 'Check it out.'

Guildenstern was addressing the royal couple. You could tell he was nervous from the strain in his voice. 'We both obey and here give up ourselves, in the full bent, to lay our service freely at your feet to be commanded.'

'What a suck-up,' said Selby.

'Come on,' said Dan. He'd spotted the exit to the main courtyard. 'The players will be arriving soon.'

6

Good Bit

Selby and Dan wound their way through a long dark corridor that eventually emerged into the main courtyard of the castle.

Hamlet was there, and so were Rosencrantz and Guildenstern.

'How did they get here before us?' asked Selby.

'It's a new scene,' said Dan. 'We've jumped ahead.' As they drew near they could hear what Hamlet was telling his friends.

'I have of late, wherefore I know not, lost all my mirth,' said Hamlet, 'forgone all custom of exercises, and indeed it goes so heavily with my disposition that this goodly frame, the earth, seems to me a sterile promontory.'

'He's describing the symptoms of depression,' said Selby.

'Yes, that's clear to us,' said Dan. 'But in Shakespeare's day there was no understanding of mental illness.'

'That must have been hard,' said Selby. 'To have strange feelings and thoughts, but no words to describe them.'

'What a piece of work is man!' continued Hamlet. 'How noble in reason, how infinite in faculty, in form and moving how express and admirable, in action how like an angel, in apprehension how like a god!'

'Is he comparing himself to a god?' asked Selby. 'That's kind of egotistical.'

'Wait for it,' said Dan. 'There's a *but* coming.'

'The beauty of the world, the paragon of animals – and yet, to me, what is this quintessence of dust? Man delights not me – no, nor woman neither.'

'Okay, that is bleak,' said Selby.

Just then, there was excited commotion over by the main gate. A group of travelling performers with carts full of props and banners were entering through the arch, heralding their own arrival by playing recorders and horns.

Hamlet went over to meet them at the gate. He actually looked happy – almost giddy with excitement. Polonius was waiting too, fussing about.

'The actors come hither my lord,' said Polonius.

'Buzz, buzz,' said Hamlet, not even looking at his uncle's bumbling advisor. He called out to the performers as they entered the courtyard, 'Y'are welcome, masters, welcome all! I am glad to see thee well. Welcome, good friends.'

The performers were a little over-awed to be met by the prince himself.

Hamlet noticed Selby approach and called out to her, 'We are in for a treat. Tonight, these excellent players will perform a scene for us.'

'Cool,' said Selby.

'Aye, cool and hot and all the emotions man can master in between,' said Hamlet. He turned to the leader of the acting troop. 'Come, give us a taste of your quality. Come, a passionate speech.'

'What speech, my good lord?' asked the actor.

'I heard thee speak me a speech once, 'twas Aeneas' tale to Dido,' said Hamlet, 'where he speaks of Priam's slaughter.'

'Is he seriously going to make this actor guy perform right now?' Selby asked Dan.

'He's a prince,' said Dan. 'He's used to getting his own way.'

The actor stepped forward and went into performance mode, his voice swelling with gravitas as he spoke . . .

PLAYER   *Anon he finds him*
Striking too short at Greeks.
His antique sword,
Rebellious to his arm, lies where
it falls,
Repugnant to command . . .

The actor was really milking it. He rolled his 'r's and elongated each vowel sound. It would have been silly if it weren't so brilliant. His voice filled the whole courtyard. He spoke with the strain of someone exhausted from fighting with a heavy sword in a long battle.

Hamlet was spellbound, hanging on the actor's every word. Selby felt herself drawn in too. She was standing in a courtyard in Denmark, but as she listened to the actor she felt sympathy with the

68

mythic warrior he portrayed – exhausted in the heat on a North African beach. It was electrifying to have an actor with a rich, powerful voice performing just a metre or two away.

> PLAYER   . . . *On Mars's armour forged for*
> *proof eterne,*
> *With less remorse than Pyrrhus'*
> *bleeding sword,*
> *Now falls on Priam.*
> *Out, out, thou strumpet of*
> *Fortune! . . .*

Dan leaned in and whispered in Selby's ear, 'Better than your daytime soap operas, hey?'

Selby elbowed him in the ribs in response. She wanted to hear the rest of the speech.

> PLAYER   . . . *In mincing with his sword her*
> *husband's limbs,*
> *The instant burst of clamour that*
> *she made,*
> *Unless things mortal move them*
> *not all,*

Would have made milch the burning
eyes of heaven,
And passion in the gods.

Hamlet had tears in his eyes as he listened. Polonius noticed this and muttered to himself, 'Look where he has not turned his colour, and has tears in's eyes.' He called out to the actor, 'Prithee, no more.'

Hamlet nodded and wiped his eyes. ''Tis well. I'll have thee speak out the rest of this soon.' He turned to Polonius, 'Good my lord, will you see the players well bestowed?'

The actors left with Polonius but Hamlet hung back. Selby went over to him, but Hamlet began talking, more to himself than to her. 'I have heard that guilty creatures sitting at a play,' he began, 'have, by the very cunning of the scene, been struck so to the soul that presently they have proclaimed their malefactions.'

'What?' said Selby, totally confused.

'He thinks he can get the actors to perform a play so moving that it will make his uncle spontaneously confess that he committed murder,' explained Dan.

'Aye, for murder, though it have no tongue, will

speak,' explained Hamlet. 'I'll have these players play something like the murder of my father before mine uncle.'

'What?' said Selby. 'Let me get this straight. You're going to put on a show that acts out that crazy poison-in-the-ear story?'

'Aye,' said Hamlet. 'Then I'll observe my uncle's looks. If he but blench, I know my course.'

'But you've already been told by the ghost of your father what happened,' said Selby. 'Isn't that enough?'

'The spirit that I have seen may be a devil,' said Hamlet, 'and the devil hath power t'assume a pleasing shape.'

'Okay,' said Selby. She wasn't terribly religious herself, but when she imagined the devil, she imagined he had better things to do with his time than impersonate ghosts.

'Yea,' continued Hamlet. 'And perhaps out of my weakness and my melancholy, as he is very potent with such spirits, abuses me to damn me.'

'He's saying he thinks the devil is taking advantage of his deep depression,' said Dan.

'Yeah, I got that,' said Selby. 'I thought psychology hadn't been invented in the sixteenth century.'

Dan shrugged. 'Shakespeare's own son died very young. Shakespeare sank into a deep depression for months, and that's when he wrote *Hamlet*. That's why there is so much stuff about death and depression, as well as fathers and sons in this play. These are auto-biographical chunks of Shakespeare's own experience, and because he was so intuitive it sounds like modern psychology. *Hamlet* actually inspired Freud when he was developing his principals of psychoanalysis.'

'The play's the thing,' said Hamlet, 'wherein I'll catch the conscience of the king.'

'That's a really crazy idea,' said Selby. 'Even *Columbo* doesn't have plots that ridiculous.'

'*Columbo*?' asked Hamlet.

'An eighties TV show,' said Selby. 'It was unusual because the audience always knew the killer at the beginning. The mystery was how Columbo would solve it.'

'I know the killer of my father,' said Hamlet.

'Yes,' agreed Selby. 'This story is similar that way.'

'You're not going to get an essay question on the parallels between *Hamlet* and *Columbo*,' said Dan.

'It's a shame,' said Selby. 'At least I'd be familiar with one of the stories.'

7

R U OK

Hamlet was very quiet as Selby and Dan walked back into the castle with him. From his silence and the scowl on his face, something was clearly churning in his mind. Selby and Dan had a lot on their minds too, so they were all quiet, locked in their own thoughts. Until Hamlet started to speak.

'To be, or not to be?' said Hamlet. 'That is the question.'

'What do you mean?' asked Selby.

'Whether 'tis nobler in the mind,' said Hamlet, growing agitated as he struggled to say exactly what he meant, 'to suffer the slings and arrows of outrageous fortune, or . . .' he broke off.

'Or what?' asked Selby.

'Or to take arms against a sea of troubles,' said Hamlet.

'What do you mean?' asked Selby.

'And by opposing,' said Hamlet, 'end them.'

'End your troubles?' said Selby. She thought she knew what he was getting at, and it was frightening her.

'To die,' said Hamlet, 'to sleep – no more; and by a sleep to say we end.'

'Suicide?' said Selby, clutching Hamlet by the arm. 'Oh no.'

''Tis a consummation devoutly to be wished,' said Hamlet. 'To die, to sleep. To sleep, perchance to dream.'

'No,' said Selby. She was so shocked. His feelings were so real. She was just a kid. She was not qualified to deal with any of this. She turned to Dan for help. 'What did they teach us in personal health?'

'Um, I don't know,' said Dan.

'I thought you were the straight-A student!' said Selby.

'There are no grades in personal health,' said Dan.

'But they talked us through what to do and what

to say if a friend is depressed and suicidal,' said Selby. 'What was it?'

'Er . . . ring the helpline?' said Dan.

'There is no telephone here,' said Selby. 'We can't ring a helpline.'

'I don't know,' said Dan.

Selby closed her eyes as she concentrated on trying to recall what they had been taught. 'Don't judge, don't criticise, listen,' recited Selby.

'Yes, I remember that,' said Dan.

'Okay, I think I've got this,' said Selby. She turned back to Hamlet. 'It is good that you are telling us this – that you are sharing how you feel. I hear you. I understand that you are in despair and you are desperate and you want the pain to go away. But what you are considering is dreadful. We need to find an alternative that is less dreadful. Let's come up with a plan, a simple plan, of what you can do instead.'

Selby gently touched Hamlet's forearm. He reacted by grabbing her in a hug – crushing her against him – and whispering in her ear, 'But in the sleep of death what dreams may come when we have shuffled off this mortal coil, must give us pause.'

'Yes,' agreed Selby. It was a struggle to speak with him squeezing her so tightly. 'That's a good point. You should pause. Take a moment. There's no rush to do anything.'

'There's the respect that makes calamity of so long life,' said Hamlet. 'For who could bear the whips and scorns of time but that the dread of something after death?'

'I know it feels that way now,' said Selby. 'But if you can get through this hour, and this day, tomorrow may be better. Focus in on this hour. Let's get through this hour.' Selby took Hamlet by the hand. 'Together we can do this.'

Hamlet looked down at their intertwined hands, then up into Selby's eyes. For Selby, it was like looking into twin pools of despair.

'Thus conscience does make cowards of us all,' said Hamlet, 'and thus the native hue of resolutions is sicklied o'er with the pale cast of thought.'

'Thinking can be a good thing,' said Selby. 'Well . . . depending on what the thoughts are.'

'You are so wise for one so fair,' said Hamlet. 'You are the star guiding my way in this night of the blackest darkness.'

Hamlet started to lean towards her. Selby knew what was happening. She'd seen this in movies. He was going to kiss her. Selby leaned back. 'This isn't a good idea.'

They were interrupted by footsteps at the far end of the corridor.

Hamlet looked up. 'Soft you now,' he whispered as he saw who it was walking towards him. 'The fair Ophelia.'

'She is very beautiful,' said Selby. She wasn't sure why she said this, but it was such a stunning fact it was hard not to voice her thoughts.

'Nymph, in thy orisons,' muttered Hamlet to himself, 'be all my sins remembered.' He let go of Selby and turned to greet Ophelia.

'Good, my lord,' Ophelia called out to him. 'How does your honour for this many a day?'

Ophelia glanced at Selby. It was a sizing-up sort of look.

'I humbly thank you, well, well, well,' said Hamlet, pulling himself together. He wiped at his eyes. He hadn't actually cried, but there had been tears welling there.

Selby took a step back because she did not want

to intrude. Talking to Ophelia might cheer Hamlet up. But as she stepped back, Selby stepped on something. Something that said, 'Ow!' She looked down to see two pairs of shoes poking out underneath the curtain. She glanced up at Hamlet. He had noticed too. There were two people hiding there, listening in. Hamlet started to look angry.

'My lord, I have remembrances of yours,' said Ophelia. She held out a handful of letters to Hamlet. 'That I have longed long to re-deliver. I pray you now receive them.'

Hamlet looked at the papers, then glanced back at the shoes beneath the tapestry.

'No, not I,' he said, loudly enough for any eavesdropper to hear. 'I never gave you aught.'

'My honoured lord!' protested Ophelia.

Selby edged over towards Dan. 'Are they Polonius's shoes?' she whispered.

'Yes, and the king's,' said Dan. 'This whole conversation is a set-up, so they can listen in to decide whether Hamlet is mad because of his love for Ophelia.'

'That is so stupid,' said Selby. 'Even my daytime soap operas have better plot ideas that that.'

'In Shakespeare's time, most of the audience at his plays would have been drunk,' said Dan, 'and there was no amplified sound. So the plotting had to be really obvious, like a pantomime, so everyone could tell what was going on.'

'And yet every line of dialogue is as confusing as a cryptic crossword,' said Selby.

'He must have known that a lot of his audience wouldn't have followed the references to Greek mythology and Roman history,' said Dan. 'I guess it doesn't matter if you don't get every line, but if you can't follow the plot, that's a problem.'

'So we have toes poking out from under a curtain,' said Selby.

Dan shrugged. They went back to listening to Ophelia and Hamlet's conversation.

'You know right well you did,' said Ophelia. 'And with them, words of so sweet breath composed as made the things more rich.'

'Get thee to a nunnery!' snapped Hamlet. Ophelia looked shocked. But Hamlet was angry and unrepentant. 'Why wouldst thou be a breeder of sinners? I am myself indifferent honest, but yet I could accuse me of such things that it were better my mother had not borne me. We are arrant knaves, all. Believe none of us.'

'O heavenly powers, restore him!' prayed Ophelia.

'I have heard of your paintings too, well enough,' continued Hamlet accusingly. 'God hath given you one face and you make yourselves another. You jig, you amble, and you lisp, you nickname God's creatures and make your wantonness your ignorance.'

'Hey, calm down,' urged Selby, stepping forward to intervene. He was scaring Ophelia.

'But she needs to know,' said Hamlet.

'Know what?' asked Ophelia.

'My wretched heart will not stay true,' said Hamlet. 'The organ beats to its own drum. When I must throw off all idle follies and devote myself to my father's service, the gods mock me. Cupid fires his weaponry on my treacherous heart by sending an angel to lead me from my path.'

'I do not understand you, my lord,' said Ophelia.

'I love another,' said Hamlet. 'A woman whose beauty and merit far outshines your superficial gloss.'

'Please don't do this,' pleaded Selby. 'Have mercy on her.'

'Why ought I be merciful?' said Hamlet. 'She has shown no mercy as she plays my heartstrings like her very own fiddle.'

'Who is she?' Ophelia. 'Who has replaced me in your affection?'

Hamlet stood back and took Selby by the hand. 'The fair mistress Selby will one day be my queen.'

Ophelia let out a wailing noise and collapsed on the ground.

'No, I won't,' said Selby, shaking his hand off.

'You are right,' said Hamlet. 'I should not make this promise while I have vowed to avenge my father.'

Ophelia was weeping so loudly now it was impossible to ignore.

'Go to, I'll no more on't,' bellowed Hamlet. He was angry with himself now as well as her. 'It hath made me mad. I say, we will have no more marriages. Those that are married already, all but one, shall live, the rest shall keep as they are. To a nunnery, go.'

Ophelia just sat there in shock and sobbed harder. So Hamlet stormed off himself.

Ophelia looked like she would weep forever. But she didn't. She suddenly launched into speech. 'Oh, what a noble mind is here o'erthrown!'

Polonius and the king emerged from behind the curtain and slipped away. It was pathetic.

'Do they think we can't see them?' asked Selby.

'I think so,' said Dan. 'It's probably a theatrical convention. If you slip away in the shadows, the audience understands that they aren't meant to be able to see you.'

'You'd think he'd comfort his daughter,' said Selby.

Dan shrugged. 'That isn't in the play.'

Ophelia looked so pathetic and distraught. Like her heart was crushed. Selby stepped forward to make some attempt to console her, but Dan touched her arm.

'I don't think she wants to be comforted by you,' he said.

'Then you do it,' said Selby.

Dan looked horrified. 'What do I say?'

'I thought you were meant to be good with words,' said Selby.

'Not when they mean something,' said Dan.

Selby shoved Dan towards Ophelia, 'Man up. She needs you. I'm going after Hamlet.' Selby jogged off in the direction he had taken.

Dan took a tentative step towards Ophelia.

'Look, you're better off without him,' said Dan. 'This is a toxic relationship for you. It's better this way.'

But Ophelia was not really listening. She was caught up in her own troubles. 'I of ladies most deject and wretched, that sucked the honey of his music vows, now see that noble and most sovereign reason, like sweet bells jangled, out of tune and harsh.'

'You're being too forgiving. Mental illness is not an excuse for rude behaviour. He's not nice to you,' said Dan. 'I know you want to give him another chance because he's a prince, which is a big deal, but that would be a hassle you'd soon get tired of.'

Ophelia slumped sideways onto one hand, so she could hold the back of her other hand against her forehead. 'Oh, woe is me,' she wailed. 'T''have seen what I have seen, see what I see.'

'Okay,' said Dan. He had no sisters. He had been raised by his father. Essentially, he had no idea how to talk to women. Except what he'd read in books. And real life wasn't like books. When a girl cried, it was wetter and snottier and so much more awkward than anything in fiction. He had no idea how to react to such wildly dramatic hysteria, but he knew he had to do his best.

Dan crouched down to put his arm around Ophelia, but this only caused Ophelia to completely break down into wracking sobs. She collapsed forward, face first on the ground. Dan had no idea how to respond to this theatrical gesture. He tried patting her on the back, but that only made Ophelia sob louder. Then suddenly, she flung herself against his chest. Dan put his arms around her and held her until her weeping started to calm, gently rubbing her back and making soothing noises.

Eventually, Ophelia loosened her hold on the front of Dan's shirt. He released his embrace. Ophelia leaned back to look up into his face. She wasn't so pretty now that she was tear-stained and red-eyed. She looked so lost. Dan wanted to comfort her, but he didn't know how – until instinct took over. He leaned forward and kissed Ophelia gently on her lips. It was brief, but Dan noted her lips tasted of the salt from her tears.

'Oh, my lord,' said Ophelia. 'I am yours.'

Dan was feeling very overwhelmed by the situation. He had never kissed anyone so blindingly pretty before. Certainly no-one fictional. He felt a surge of exhilaration. But then his brain kicked in and he processed what Ophelia had just said.

'I beg your pardon?' asked Dan.

'My heart is yours forevermore,' said Ophelia.

'Whoa,' said Dan. 'No, that's not what I meant.'

'Your lips, spoke your promise,' said Ophelia. 'And mine do answer yes, a thousand times yes. You will mend my wounded heart with your gentle, tender affections.'

'No, you misunderstand,' said Dan.

'There is no misunderstanding a kiss, my lord,' said Ophelia. ''Tis clear enough. My father will be astonished when you call upon him. But I will vouchsafe my love and he will learn to regard you as a second son of his heart.'

'I'm only eighteen,' said Dan. 'I'm too young to get married.'

'I am but sixteen, yet I am ready to pledge my life to thine,' said Ophelia.

'This can't happen,' said Dan.

'My lord, you will not betray me and leave my reputation to certain ruin?' said Ophelia. 'To be condemned, shunned by all, for being a temptress of men.'

'No,' said Dan. 'No, that's not what I meant.'

'Then you shall go directly to my father,' said Ophelia, 'and request his blessing.'

'I think we're rushing into this,' said Dan. 'You've only just broken up with Hamlet.'

'Do not speak his name to me,' said Ophelia. 'I see now he only ever showed me a false face. But yours is a truer heart.'

8

The Play Within a Play

Dan hurried to the great hall to find Selby. When he got there he didn't recognise it at first – the room had been transformed. The cavernous space was dark except for a simple stage, which was lit with candles. The performers were acting out a silent pantomime before the main play. The king and queen and their courtiers were arranged in an audience, watching. Dan spotted Selby in the shadows, at the back of the audience, sitting with Hamlet.

Dan crept over. He didn't want to draw attention to himself. He tapped Selby on the shoulder. She flinched and turned. Hamlet glared at him. Dan tilted his head to indicate he wanted her to follow him outside. Selby looked at him like he was nuts.

She pointed to the actors on stage. The king and queen were only a few metres away. She did not want to disturb them. Dan leaned in and whispered urgently, 'We've got to get out of here!'

Selby's brow furrowed, as if to say, 'What?'

Dan beckoned to her to follow him. Selby got up and went with him into the darkness at the very back of the room, where they would be out of earshot.

'We need to leave now,' said Dan. 'Come on!'

Selby didn't move. 'But you're the one who wanted to stay,' she said.

'It's not safe here for us,' said Dan. 'Not for me anyway.' He glanced over his shoulder checking that Ophelia wasn't close by.

'What are you talking about?' said Selby. 'You're the one who said this was a once-in-a-lifetime learning opportunity, more meaningful than anything we could ever experience at home.'

'It's getting a bit too meaningful,' said Dan. 'Ophelia thinks I'm going to marry her.'

Selby let out a bark of laughter.

The audience turned. A courtier shushed her. Dan drew Selby out through the doorway and into a passageway beyond where they'd be able to talk at a more normal volume.

'She was crying,' said Dan. 'I gave her a hug and apparently that's the same as a marriage proposal for nobility in sixteenth century Denmark.'

'A hug?' said Selby.

'And a very small kiss,' conceded Dan.

'Oh, Dan,' said Selby. 'You're well-read. You should know better. That *is* a marriage proposal in the sixteenth century.'

'I wasn't thinking,' said Dan.

'No kidding,' said Selby.

Dan looked so dejected.

'Look, you should think about this,' said Selby. 'Why don't you marry her?'

'Don't be ridiculous!' said Dan.

'Everything about this situation is ridiculous,' said Selby. 'Why not lean into it? You like her. She is smart, kind and beautiful. You love it here. You could marry her and live the rest of your life inside this play.'

'I'm black,' said Dan. 'That's going to cause problems sooner or later.'

'Othello was black,' said Selby. 'And he was in a Shakespeare play.'

'Othello died,' said Dan. 'After murdering his wife. Cleopatra was Greek-African and she died after watching her husband die. Shylock was Jewish and he was stripped of all his wealth and charged with attempted murder. Ethnically diverse people do not do well in Shakespearean plays.'

'Maybe it's your job to change all that,' said Selby.

'But I don't want to get married!' said Dan.

'Not ever?' asked Selby.

'Not to Ophelia,' said Dan. 'She's really clingy.'

'To be fair, all the men in her life are horrible,' said Selby. 'It's no wonder she has issues.'

'Please, this isn't a joke,' said Dan. 'I've got to get out of here.'

'But we can't leave,' said Selby. 'Hamlet and Ophelia are both a mess. What will happen to them if we walk away now?'

'Well, Ophelia will go mad and drown when she falls in the river,' said Dan. 'And Hamlet will die in a sword fight with Laertes.'

'Wow, that's really bad!' said Selby. 'I thought Hamlet was about to be sent off to England.'

'He never gets there,' said Dan.

'We can't just walk away and let them both die,' said Selby.

'But they're fictional,' said Dan.

Selby knew this was true, but it that didn't make it right. 'They don't feel fictional,' she said. 'In this world, they are as real as us. This is reality for them.'

'If this is their reality then we should leave them to it,' said Dan.

'No,' said Selby. 'That's just wrong. Letting someone die when you know you could prevent it is wrong.'

'Who made you the Queen of Morality and Ethics,' said Dan.

'It's not complicated,' said Selby. 'It's instinctive. Letting a person die is wrong. It feels wrong.'

'If we stay here, we could end up dead too,' said Dan. 'Do you know what the death rate is in this play for the leading characters? One hundred per cent! They all die. If we become characters, we'll become a part of that.'

'Doing the wrong thing because it's easier is just cowardice,' said Selby.

'I can't die here,' said Dan. 'Who will look after my dad? What will happen to your parents? It would break their hearts if you just went missing and never went back.'

Selby imagined her mum. She might be angry with her mum now, but that would only make it worse if she went missing. It would make her mum feel guilty as well as heartbroken. It made Selby feel guilty to make her mother feel guilty. That wouldn't be fair. Then Selby had an idea.

'Let's take him with us,' said Selby.

'What?' said Dan.

'Let's take Hamlet with us,' said Selby. 'Back to the bookstore. If he leaves the narrative, he won't drive Ophelia nuts. He won't kill anyone.'

'But what would we do with him?' asked Dan.

'I don't know,' said Selby. 'But if he stays here, he's going to die anyway.'

'That's a crazy idea,' said Dan.

'I know you don't want to marry Ophelia,' said Selby. 'But if we don't do something she is going to die soon. Do you want that on your conscience?'

'No,' conceded Dan.

'Then what's the alternative?' asked Selby. 'I suppose we could take Ophelia with us, but then you'd definitely have to marry her.'

92

'Okay, fine,' said Dan. 'We'll take Hamlet.'

'Good decision,' said Selby. 'Let's get him.'

They went back to the great hall. The play was in full swing. An actor dressed up like a king was lying on a bench.

'What's happening?' whispered Selby.

'This is the re-enactment,' said Dan. 'They're going to act out the murder of Hamlet's father.'

'We're supposed to be watching how the king reacts,' said Selby. She looked across at Claudius. His face was unnaturally impassive.

'What do you call the play?' Claudius asked Hamlet.

'*The Mousetrap*,' said Hamlet.

Claudius's head whipped round, as if to gauge whether his stepson's words had a hidden meaning.

On stage, another actor entered, carrying a jug. He went over to the player king and held up the jug in a theatrical gesture, to show the audience.

'Thou mixture rank, or midnight weeds collected,' said the actor, talking to the jug itself. 'On wholesome life usurp immediately.' Then he poured the poison in the sleeping king's ear.

Hamlet turned to his mother and stepfather and

explained the plot loudly. 'A poisons him i'th'garden for's estate.' He stared into his stepfather's eyes. 'You shall see anon how the murderer gets the love of Gonzago's wife.'

Claudius shot to his feet. He was quivering with emotion. It was not clear if it was rage or fear – most likely both. He looked like he had seen a ghost.

'Give me some light.' ordered Claudius.

Servants hurried to light torches.

'Away!' barked Claudius as he stormed out, all his entourage following with him.

Hamlet was delighted, like a child who had carried out a prank. He was quivering with excitement as he walked over to Selby and Dan. 'Oh, good Selby, I'll take the ghost's word for a thousand pound,' said Hamlet. 'Didst perceive?'

'Yeah, I saw it,' said Selby.

'Upon the talk of the poisoning?' said Hamlet.

'He didn't take that well,' said Selby.

Rosencrantz and Guildenstern entered from a side door and beckoned to Hamlet.

'Ah, I must see what yonder fools require,' said Hamlet. He left Selby and Dan to talk among themselves.

'So that's it?' said Selby. 'Claudius did kill his brother?'

Dan nodded.

'Now Hamlet knows the truth, what's he going to do?' asked Selby.

'This is the bit where you get to see Hamlet's main character flaw,' said Dan. 'He can't make a decision.'

'I guess if you're having mental health problems it's hard to think clearly,' said Selby. 'We should talk to him before he does something rash.'

They turned around. Rosencrantz and Guilden-stern were still there, but Hamlet was nowhere to be seen.

'Where did he go?' asked Selby.

'Oh no,' said Dan.

'What now?' asked Selby.

'There's a scene coming up,' said Dan, 'where Hamlet confronts his mother.'

'So?' asked Selby.

'It's the first death of the play,' said Dan.

'Come on,' said Selby. 'We've got to find them.'

They both took off running.

9

Things Turn Nasty

As they ran up the main staircase, Dan and Selby could hear shouting. It was Hamlet. 'Mother, you have my father much offended!' he bellowed.

'We've got to stop him,' said Selby.

Selby rushed down the long corridor. The door to the queen's bedroom was hanging open. When Selby burst in, what she saw was shocking. Hamlet held the queen by her arms. The queen looked distressed. Hamlet was ranting and out of control.

'Come, come and sit you down. You shall not budge!' ordered Hamlet, shoving his mother so she fell backwards onto the bed.

'Stop it!' cried Selby.

But Hamlet was raving with anger. His face was

red, the veins in his neck were bulging and spittle flew out of his mouth as he shouted at his mother, 'You go not till I set you up a glass where you may see the inmost part of you.' Hamlet turned to find a mirror.

The queen looked terrified. It was horrible to see a woman who, as queen, usually had such composure and dignity, being treated with so little respect.

'What wilt thou do?' asked the queen. She was trembling with fear. 'Thou wilt not murder me?'

Hamlet did not respond. He was too busy dragging a large mirror across the room. The queen apparently thought he did intend to murder her. 'Help, help ho!' she cried out in desperation.

A voice came from behind the curtains. 'What ho! Help, help, help!'

Hamlet spun around, drawing his sword and facing the sound. He realised there was someone hiding behind the cloth. 'How now, a rat? Dead for a ducat, dead!'

Hamlet lunged toward the curtain, but Selby dived forward and caught his arm.

'No!' she cried. 'You'll kill him.'

'That is my object, lady,' declared Hamlet. 'Unhand me.'

'Selby, what are you doing?' called Dan, but he couldn't move to help her because on seeing another man enter her bedroom, the queen had run to Dan for protection, collapsing in his arms.

Hamlet tried to shake Selby off, but, unlike the queen, Selby was used to roughhousing with siblings. Selby hugged Hamlet's arm tight into her armpit, squeezing it to the side of her chest. She couldn't make Hamlet let go of the sword, but she could hold on to his sword arm so he couldn't move freely. 'You'll regret it. You can't unkill a man. You'll set off a chain of events that will end tragically for everyone.'

'Not I!' declared Hamlet. 'Unhand me now!'

Selby tightened her grip. The sword was held fast. She could feel the initial surge of rage starting to seep out of Hamlet. When suddenly – Polonius burst out from behind the curtain and ran straight into Hamlet's outstretched blade.

'Aaagh!' cried Polonius.

'Oh my God,' said Selby, letting go of Hamlet's arm.

Hamlet was shocked to find Polonius impaled on his sword. He drew the blade out of the old man's chest and Polonius collapsed on the ground.

'Oh me!' cried the distraught queen. 'What hast thou done?' She collapsed to her knees, pulling Dan down with her.

Hamlet was too shocked to comprehend. 'Nay, I know not. Is it the king?'

'You thought it was your uncle behind the curtain?' asked Selby.

'Aye,' said Hamlet.

'Oh, I am slain,' whimpered Polonius. He struggled for breath. The blood from whatever internal injury he had suffered was on his lips. After one final shuddering half breath, he was dead.

'Oh no,' said Selby. 'This is really bad.'

'Thou wretched rash, intruding fool, farewell,' said Hamlet, shaking his head. 'I took thee for thy better.'

Selby grabbed Hamlet's arm and shook it. 'This is why you need to make sure you know who you're about to kill before you kill them!'

'I thought you were anti-violence,' said Dan from the side of the room, where he was still propping up the queen.

'I'm also anti-stupidity,' said Selby.

Hamlet turned on his mother. He was still really angry with her. He didn't spare a beat to be remorseful over what he had just done. 'Sit you down,' he ordered his mother. 'And let me wring your heart, for so I shall. If it be made of penetrable stuff. If damned custom have not brassed it so, that it be proof and bulwark against sense.'

'Hey, stop that!' said Selby, whacking Hamlet on the shoulder to get his attention.

'Definitely getting over your aversion to violence now,' said Dan.

'Be quiet, you're not helping,' said Selby, before turning back to Hamlet. 'You can't talk to your mother that way. It's no way for a son to behave, no matter what she's done.'

'Yay, what have I done, that thous dar'st wag thy tongue in noise so rude against me?' asked the queen.

Dan sighed and braced himself for the onslaught he had read many times in the play. 'You shouldn't have asked,' he said.

Because now, Hamlet really started yelling. 'Such an act that blurs the grace and blush of modesty!' He waved his arms about as he struggled to find words big enough to encapsulate his feelings. 'Call virtue hypocrite, takes off the rose from the fair forehead of an innocent love and sets a blister there, makes marriage vows as false as dicers' oaths.'

'Enough!' yelled Selby, picking up a jug of water from the bedside table and throwing it in Hamlet's face. Unfortunately, her hand slipped on the handle and the whole jug flew out of her grip, hitting Hamlet on the nose. His head jolted back from the blow. The jug and its contents smashed at his feet on the floor.

'Whoops, sorry about that,' said Selby.

Hamlet staggered backwards. It had been a heavy jug. He was finally stunned into silence. Selby took advantage of the opportunity to say what she wanted to say. 'You can't speak to a woman that way, let alone your mother. You should be ashamed of yourself. Where I come from, your mother could get an apprehended violence order against you for the way you're behaving.'

Hamlet drew breath to argue back, but then suddenly fell silent. At first Selby thought he was listening, but then she realised he was looking at something behind her. Selby felt the awful sense of dread that had affected her when she was up on the castle walls. She turned to see the ghost – Hamlet's father.

The old king was an ethereal spectre, made up of nothing more solid than light and shadow. He walked into the centre of the room, but he was clearly dead and it was horrible to behold – like he was decaying before their eyes. The room seemed to grow cold with his presence.

Hamlet recoiled in fear, 'A king of shreds and patches. Save me and hover o'er me with your wings, you heavenly guards! What would your gracious figure?'

'Alas, he's mad,' said the queen. She was glancing from Hamlet to where Hamlet was looking – but from the way her eyes roved about, she clearly could not see the ghost herself.

'You can say that again,' agreed Dan. He still hung onto the queen in case she fainted, and perhaps a bit for support himself. It was chilling to be in the room with the rotting spectre of the ghost.

'Do you not come your tardy son to chide?' Hamlet asked the ghost. It was weird to see Hamlet regress into a childish tone. He was manly and confident enough when talking to everyone else, but apparently with his own father he would be forever trapped as a disappointing young son. He practically writhed at the ghost's feet. 'That, lapsed in time and passion, let's go by th'important acting of your dread command? Oh say!'

'Do not forget,' the ghost commanded in a slow quavering voice. 'This visitation is but to whet thy almost blunted purpose.'

Hamlet cowered away. But the ghost was not paying attention. He was distracted by the sight of his widow. He walked away from Hamlet and towards her, where she cowered in Dan's arms. The dead king was clearly heartbroken to see her so distressed. 'But look, amazement on thy mother sits.' The ghost reached out to comfort her, but the queen could not see or hear him. There was nothing he could do. The ghost turned back to Hamlet. 'Oh, step between her and her fighting soul. Conceit in weakest bodies strongest works. Speak to her, Hamlet.'

'Yes, that's right,' said Selby. 'Your dad specifically said not to be mean to your mother, and you've done the opposite. Make it up to her.'

Hamlet stepped closer to his mother. 'How is it with you, lady?' he asked awkwardly, attempting to put his emotions in reverse, and not succeeding entirely.

'Alas, how is it with you, that you do bend your eyes on vacancy?' asked the queen. She was, after all, his mother. She had already forgiven his bad behaviour and was concerned now with the sanity of her beloved only son. She let go of Dan and moved towards Hamlet. 'To whom do you speak this?'

'Do you see nothing there?' asked Hamlet, pointing to the ghost.

'No, nothing but ourselves,' said the queen.

'Why, look you there! Look how it steals away,' said Hamlet, watching the ghost trudge towards the doorway. 'My father in his habit as he lived. Look where he goes, even now, out at the portal.'

'This is the very coinage of your brain,' said the queen, shaking her head sadly.

'It is not madness that I have uttered,' Hamlet assured her, now showing a glimpse of normal affection. 'Mother, for love of grace, lay not that flattering unction to your soul that not your trespass but my madness speaks.'

'Oh, Hamlet,' said the queen, stroking her son's face, 'thou has cleft my heart in twain.'

'Oh, throw away the worser part of it, and live the purer with the other half,' urged Hamlet. He had calmed down and was regarding his mother with affection again.

'Be thou assured,' said the queen, tears now streaming down her face, 'if words be made of breath, and breath of life, I have no life to breathe what thou hast said to me.'

Now finally, Hamlet looked in part remorseful. 'I must to England, you know that?' he said.

'Alack, I had forgot,' said the queen, clutching her head. ''Tis so concluded on.'

'This man shall set me packing,' said Hamlet, indicating Polonius dead upon the floor. It was a sobering sight. Selby had never seen a dead body before. There was so much blood, pooling on the floor and soaking into his clothes. Polonius looked so old. He had been pathetic in life. He was even more so now.

Hamlet stood up and grabbed hold of the body. 'I'll lug the guts into the neighbour room. Mother, good night. Indeed, this counsellor is now most still, most secret, and most grave who was in life a foolish prating knave.' Hamlet started dragging Polonius out. As soon as he was gone from sight the queen collapsed on the bed weeping.

'What a mess,' said Selby.

'We'd better get out of here,' said Dan. 'The king is going to enter next.'

It felt wrong to leave the queen, but they couldn't be discovered in her bedroom, and her husband would look after her.

Selby followed Dan out of the room. They caught a glimpse of Hamlet at the end of the corridor, dragging Polonius around a corner. 'This is like a French farce, people coming and going and hiding behind curtains,' said Selby.

'It's not very funny for Polonius,' said Dan.

'No . . . why am I wet?' asked Selby, reaching around to touch the back of her sweater. When she drew her hand back, it was red. 'Oh gross, I've got blood on my shirt! That's never going to come out.'

'Like Lady Macbeth,' said Dan.

'What?' asked Selby.

'"Out, out, damn spot,"' quoted Dan. 'It's from *Macbeth*, you know, another Shakespeare play. She gets blood on her hands and can't clean it off.'

'I haven't read that one either,' said Selby.

'You might want to skip it. It's even grimmer than this one,' said Dan.

'I can't wear this,' said Selby. She took off her sweater, but then didn't know where to put it.

'Don't just drop it,' said Dan. 'It's evidence. The last thing we need is you being accused of Polonius's murder. You'd better burn it. Here, put this on.' He took off his own jacket.

'Now you'll get cold,' said Selby. Dan only had a t-shirt on underneath and they were in Denmark in an unheated castle. It was pretty nippy.

'I didn't just accidentally get involved in a stabbing,' said Dan. 'I'm less likely to go into shock.'

'How does Hamlet get out of this one?' asked Selby.

'The king has arranged to have him sent off to England with Rosencrantz and Guildenstern,' said Dan.

'After all this, he does have to get rid of Hamlet,' said Selby. 'At least he doesn't kill him.'

'Well . . . he tries. The king sends a letter with Rosencrantz and Guildenstern to the English king, asking *him* to kill Hamlet,' said Dan.

'Wow!' said Selby. 'Worst stepdad ever.'

'But Hamlet finds the letter,' said Dan. 'And forges

a replacement letter, asking the King of England to kill Rosencrantz and Guildenstern instead.'

'And that's how those two twits are going to die?' asked Selby.

'Yep,' said Dan.

'That's terrible,' said Selby. 'They might be misguided, but they don't deserve the death penalty.'

'Lots of people die in this play who don't deserve to,' said Dan.

'If we don't intervene now, this is going to be a bloodbath, isn't it?' said Selby.

'Well, how do you classify a bloodbath?' asked Dan.

'Three or more people dead,' said Selby.

Dan counted on his hands. 'Yeah, then it's a bloodbath. The death count is more than twice that.'

'Let's kidnap him,' said Selby.

'Who? Hamlet?' asked Dan.

'Yeah,' said Selby.

'You can't kidnap the Prince of Denmark!' said Dan.

'Of course we can,' said Selby. 'People used to do things like that to royalty all the time. Besides, he's just a man. We shouldn't be in awe of him because he's royalty. We should just do it. It would be undemocratic not to.'

'But how?' asked Dan.

'I'll bop him on the head,' said Selby. She looked about for something to use. There was a dish on the nearby table. 'This will do the trick.'

'You can't do that!' exclaimed Dan.

'Here he comes now,' said Selby.

She had spotted Hamlet striding towards them, carrying a bag.

'Hamlet, pray tell,' said Selby. 'What be that o'er yonder?' She pointed to a window behind Hamlet. Hamlet turned to look and Selby whacked him on the back of the head with the bowl. He collapsed.

'This is bad, very bad,' said Dan.

'Grab a foot,' urged Selby as she picked one up herself.

'Where are we taking him?' asked Dan.

'To the bookstore,' said Selby.

'What?' said Dan.

'We've got to get him up to the battlements so we can get him through the portal,' said Selby.

'If you wanted to try that, why didn't you lure

him up there, then knock him out?' asked Dan. 'Now we've got to drag him up a spiral staircase.'

'Okay, that was silly,' conceded Selby. Looking at Hamlet slumped on the floor, she realised how solidly he was built. 'It must be the air here. It makes people violent.'

10

Kidnapping Through
Alternate Realities

Twenty minutes later, Dan and Selby finally dragged Hamlet up the last flight of stairs. They both collapsed, gasping for breath.

'That is worse . . . than anything . . . I've ever . . . had to do . . . in PE,' said Dan between gulping in air.

'It's funny, all the stupid things they make you do in PE,' said Selby. 'They really should teach you dragging skills. The ability to drag another human is important. You might need to do it to rescue someone from a house fire. Or get a sick person in a car and drive them to hospital.'

'Or get a fictional person into the real world so they won't go on a killing spree,' said Dan.

'It sounds silly when you put it that way,' said Selby.

'It doesn't feel silly,' said Dan. 'Between the stitch in my side and the fear of being discovered by a murderous monarch while we're kidnapping a member of his royal family, nothing about this feels frivolous at all.'

'Come on, let's shove him through,' said Selby. 'Before we think too much and convince ourselves to do something even more stupid.' Selby got up and dragged Hamlet closer to the portal.

'What if this doesn't work?' asked Dan.

'I haven't considered that option,' admitted Selby.

Dan paused. 'And what if it *does* work?' asked Dan. 'What are we going to do with him on the other side?'

'I haven't considered that option either,' admitted Selby. She rested Hamlet's weight against her legs for a moment while she shook out her arms. 'But staying here is definitely not going to work. The death count will be too high. If he does go through, the first thing we should do is get him medical attention, I suppose.'

'For the head injury,' said Dan.

'Well, yes, that,' said Selby. 'But I was thinking

more for the delusions, morbid fantasies and violent tendencies.'

'Urgh, who goes there,' muttered Hamlet, his eyes fluttering open.

'He's coming round,' said Dan.

'Quick,' said Selby. 'Pull him through. I'll push.'

Dan had his back to the portal. He stepped backwards and his leg disappeared. He pulled Hamlet and they both began to pass through. Selby pushed Hamlet's legs. In a moment, they were entirely gone. Selby was alone on the battlements. The cold wind bit at her face. The night sky was black and empty. Selby realised she was in sixteenth century Denmark and she was totally alone – in every sense. She had always felt alone in life. But nothing could be more alone than this. Suddenly – a hand reached back and grasped her wrist. Dan's face emerged. 'Come on, you're not leaving me to deal with him alone,' he pulled Selby's arm. She lurched forward and she started to fall, she could hear her own voice again.

. . . Alas poor Yorick! I knew him, Horatio . . .
. . . The lady doth protest too much . . .
. . . Neither a borrower nor a lender be . . .

Then the next thing she knew, Selby was lying on the floor of the bookstore. She took a deep breath. It was home. It smelled like home. Dan was standing over her smiling. 'You made it.'

After the wind on the battlements, it was so quiet and warm. Even the carpet under her back was comforting and soft compared to the stone floors of the castle.

'I did,' agreed Selby. She turned to see Hamlet, Prince of Denmark, sitting just a couple of metres away, leaning against the cooking section.

'What on earth are you doing?' accused Mum. She had just rounded the biography stack and was scowling.

'Mum!' cried Selby. She leapt to her feet and gave her a big hug.

'What's going on?' demanded Mum. Selby was not normally a hugger. 'What's gotten into you?' She looked at Selby suspiciously.

'We're just ... um ... enacting a scene from *Hamlet*, Mrs Michaels,' improvised Dan.

'Oh,' said Mum. She eyed Hamlet uncertainly. Apart from wearing period costume, he was as dishevelled as a person would be if they'd been bopped on the head and dragged up a spiral stair-case. 'Well, get up off the floor. You'll frighten the customers.'

'Pardon my behaviour,' said Hamlet, 'My legs will not obey me at present.'

Selby looked around, 'What customers?'

'The ones we'd have if your friend wasn't lying on the floor,' snapped Mum. 'And who is this anyway? Is he drunk?'

'No, he just bumped his head,' explained Dan. 'Ha–rrison is a friend from my book club . . .' Apparently, Dan had a gift for fiction. 'He is a great Shakespeare enthusiast. He has all the costumes and he knows all about *Hamlet*. I asked for his help getting Selby to understand the motivations of the character.'

'Oh, well . . . that's nice,' said Mum, thawing a little. She instinctively didn't like the look of the young man slumped on the floor of her bookstore. But she was such a literature snob that, to her mind, anyone who liked Shakespeare couldn't be that bad. 'How is the study coming along?'

'Very good,' said Selby. 'I know a lot more about the play than I did.'

'Really?' asked Mum. 'Let's see about that ...' She crossed her arms and eyed Selby. 'Is the ghost real, or a figment of Hamlet's unstable mind?'

'Unstable mind?' interrupted Hamlet. 'Who dare say this?' He tried to get to his feet and stumbled.

'Whoa, steady there, big fella,' said Dan, grabbing hold of Hamlet as he tried to rise.

'Real,' said Selby. 'Horatio, Marcellus and Barnardo see the ghost too.'

Mum nodded. She was impressed. But she wasn't done with her test questions. 'What is the significance of the flowers Ophelia picks when she goes mad?' asked Mum.

'Ophelia, mad?! What lies are these?' demanded Hamlet. Dan kept a firm hold of him.

'We're not up to that bit yet,' said Selby.

'That is late in act four, Mrs Michaels,' said Dan. 'Selby is up to act three. She's done really well for one session.'

'Mrs Michaels?' said Hamlet. His face lit up. He asked Selby, 'Is this good lady your mother?'

'Um, yes,' said Selby, glancing at Mum.

Hamlet straightened and, through this simple act of adjusting his body language, he took on the persona

116

of a European prince, not just a student who'd been sprawled on the floor. He bowed to Mum. 'Madam, it is my honour to meet you.'

'Yes, well, that's all right,' said Mum, still suspicious that this young person was teasing her. 'You can stay if you're a friend of Dan's.' Selby noted that she didn't say 'a friend of Selby's'.

'My good lady,' said Hamlet, addressing Mum formally, 'I must inform you, because deception would go against my honour, that I come to you not as a mere acquaintance.'

'You don't?' said Mum.

'I hold your daughter in the highest esteem,' said Hamlet. 'She is the most beautiful creature I have ever laid eyes on.'

'Is he on drugs?' asked Mum, turning on Selby.

'Aye, well may you ask if I am inebriated,' said Hamlet, taking Selby by the hand and looking lovingly at her face. 'I feel bewitched when I look upon her. But I have not drunk of Rhenish wine or a sorceress's brew. It is herself I love. And not just her beauty in person which I admire, but her wisdom of heart. I intend, God willing, and with the permission of your good husband, to make her my wife.'

117

'Urgh,' groaned Selby.

Dan smothered a laugh.

'This is so embarrassing,' muttered Selby.

Mum's eyes narrowed. She definitely thought Hamlet was messing with her now. 'I've said you can stay. Don't push your luck.'

'I give you thanks, good lady,' said Hamlet bowing again. 'I shall do nothing to make you regret your decision.'

Mum glowered for a long moment. She was clearly considering changing her mind and throwing him out anyway. 'Fine,' she eventually said. 'But no more sprawling on the floor.'

'Upon my honour, it will be thus,' said Hamlet, laying his hand across his heart as if it were a solemn oath.

Mum glared at him one more time and left them to it.

'I see from whence your fighting spirit springs,' said Hamlet. 'A proud lady is your mother, and with good reason, with such a precious child to protect.'

'Yeah, that's one spin on it,' said Selby.

'You better go and change,' Dan told her.

'Why?' asked Selby.

'You've got Polonius's blood on your jeans,' said Dan.

Selby looked down. A wave of nausea washed over her. She had seen a man die just moments ago. She realised she was shivering. She hadn't noticed before. If she had, she would have assumed it was the cold in Denmark. But the shop was warm. It must be shock.

'I'll take a shower,' said Selby. 'Keep an eye on him. I'll be as quick as I can.'

11

Hamlet, Prince of the Bookstore

When Selby headed back to the bookstore, she was feeling more her old self again. Showered and warm, and wearing fresh clothes – all that had happened felt more like a dream. But as soon as she came down the stairs into the stockroom at the back of the shop, the dream came crashing back into her reality again. She could hear Hamlet out in the store. He was clearly talking to a customer.

'You read books with coloured pictures?' said Hamlet. 'Prithee tell me, is thy school so lacklustre that they've failed to teach you letters?'

Selby stepped out onto the shop floor and saw that he was talking to two teenage boys.

'It's called a graphic novel,' said the teen.

'Terminology does not increase its literary merit,' said Hamlet. 'My lad, to better yourself, you must read books by the greats.'

'It is great,' protested the teenager.

'Nay, in this, you are wrong,' said Hamlet, leading them to the classics section. 'All that you need know of mankind and his many follies can be learned from this text.'

He picked out a book and handed it to the teenager.

'Plooo-tar-ch.' The boy attempted to read the title.

'Plutarch,' Hamlet corrected him.

The boy flicked through the pages.

'It looks boring,' said the boy.

'Nonsense,' said Hamlet. 'These pages capture man's very essence.'

'Does it have action?' asked the teen.

'Or zombies?' asked his friend.

Hamlet snatched the book out of his hands. 'Get thee gone. You are not worthy of literature. The hours your tutor spent teaching you to read were in vain. Education is wasted on one such as you.'

The teenagers stood frozen.

'Get thee gone, I say!' bellowed Hamlet, whacking the boy on the shoulder with the copy of Plutarch.

'Ow!' cried the boy.

'That's assault,' accused his friend.

'Indeed it is!' agreed Hamlet, whacking him too. 'Just as talking with you is an assault upon mine ears.'

'I'll just get the graphic novel then,' said the boy.

'Never! There will be no books for you,' declared Hamlet, snatching the graphic novel out of his hands. 'Your shameless ignorance makes a mockery of this fine institution. Go – stand on the street where you belong!' He whacked the boy again for good measure.

'I'm telling the police you hit me,' complained the boy.

'Excellent!' said Hamlet. 'The police will have a sturdy stick with which to beat you harder.'

The boys scurried away.

'I like your new friend,' said Dad. He was watching from behind the counter, grinning from ear to ear.

'He just scared off two customers,' said Selby.

'Those boys never spend their money on books,' said Dad. 'They just stand and read them in the store.'

'Still,' said Selby. 'He hit them.'

'I wish I had the courage to do that too,' said Dad wistfully.

'You can't beat the customers,' said Selby.

'I've often wanted to,' said Dad.

'What have you there, good woman,' Hamlet asked, approaching Mrs Tink, who was looking at the novels in the romance section. 'Egad! A story of romance? I beg you – do not indulge in this foul bilge.'

'I like romance,' said Mrs Tink.

'Then you enjoy delusion?' asked Hamlet. 'For the happiness of man and woman bound together is a notion built on nothing but deceit. A fairytale used to beguile the common populace.'

'It's cheerful,' argued Mrs Tink.

'But what right have we to good cheer?' asked Hamlet. 'When we are surrounded by so much devilry.'

'It's because of all the devilry that I'd rather read a romance,' said Mrs Tink.

'My good woman,' said Hamlet. 'Then this book is no more to you than a tankard of ale to a drunk.'

'I like drinking wine when I read them too,' said Mrs Tink.

'Then thou art a sop twice over,' said Hamlet.

'You are very rude,' accused Mrs Tink.

'That is what the Greeks told Socrates,' said Hamlet, 'right before they sentenced him to death for his honesty.'

'So you're saying, I shouldn't get the book?' asked Mrs Tink.

'Nay, not at all,' said Hamlet. 'To sleep away thy waking hours is a sweet pastime for those whose muted conscience allows such unchecked folly.'

'That'll be $15.99, Mrs Tink,' said Mum, taking the book out of her hand before Mrs Tink could change her mind, or Hamlet could hit her with it. Mum still had some semblance of capitalist drive.

'Oh, and I believe,' Dad said, throwing his arm around Selby's shoulders, 'that I must congratulate you on your upcoming marriage.'

'What?' said Selby in alarm.

'Hamlet has asked my permission to wed you,' said Dad. 'And, of course, I agreed.'

'You didn't?' said Selby.

'Well, none of my children are interested in working in the bookstore,' said Dad. 'I'd be delighted to have a son-in-law who is so keen to advise my customers.'

'This is all a big joke to you, isn't it?' said Selby.

'I see it more as an act of performance art,' said Dad.

'I'll take him over to Dan's house to get him out of your way,' said Selby.

'You will not,' said Dad. 'His shift doesn't finish until six pm.'

'You've given him a job!' exclaimed Selby.

'He read a fourteenth century Nordic folktale to Mrs Haversham and made her cry, it was so beautiful,' said Dad. 'Your fiancée will be a drawcard for our store. I'm going to get him to do the toddler story time on Friday.'

'You're as nuts as he is,' said Selby.

'You can't work in the book trade unless you are, dear,' said Dad.

Selby went looking for Dan. She found him sitting in the children's section, reading from their copy of *Hamlet*.

'What are you sitting around for?' asked Selby. 'You've got to get him out of here.'

'It was your idea to bring him back to the bookstore,' said Dan. 'What did you think was going to happen?'

'Not this,' said Selby. 'I didn't think my parents were going to love him like a second son.'

'Are you jealous?' he asked.

'Yes!' said Selby. 'He is four hundred years old, Danish and fictional, and he has more in common with my parents than I do.'

'Look, things will settle,' said Dan. 'Hamlet will calm down. The novelty will wear off. He'll assimilate to this world in time. I'll take him to work with me tomorrow. He won't be able to get into too much trouble helping to rewire Mrs Ahyong's granny flat. Get a good night's sleep. You've got school tomorrow. When you get home, we'll figure out a way to make this work.'

'If he hasn't stabbed anyone before then,' said Selby. 'He's still carrying that sword. It's probably still covered in Polonius's blood.'

'There you go,' said Dan. 'If he gets really annoying, we can report him to the police. Being fictional Danish royalty won't help him here.'

Selby thought about everything Dan had said. She couldn't see any alternative, but perhaps that was because she was so exhausted. Travelling through a portal in the space-time-fiction continuum and inadvertently getting involved in manslaughter was physically and emotionally draining. She really needed sleep.

'But where is he going to stay?' asked Selby. 'He can't stay here in the flat with me and Mum and Dad. He thinks he's in love with me. It would be awkward.'

'I'll take him back to my place,' said Dan. 'Dad won't mind. I'll tell Hamlet it's only proper, that he can't stay under the same roof as you until you're wed.'

'Don't you start too,' said Selby. 'It's not funny.'

'Yes, it is,' said Dan. 'Just not for you.'

'I'm going to bed,' said Selby.

'Goodnight, sweet future princess,' said Dan.

'Whatever,' said Selby, as she turned to trudge back upstairs.

12

To Be, or Not to Be... A Pain in the Butt

When Selby got up the following morning, the whole previous day felt totally unreal. She knew it wasn't, because she still had a bruise on her shin from the spiral staircase and one under her arm from trying to wrestle the sword out of Hamlet's hand. It was such a relief to be going to school. She never thought she would feel that way about school but it was true. At least at school there were no death threats. Well ... Mr Sophocles may have mentioned the death penalty for anyone who didn't hand in their history homework, but she assumed that was hyperbole.

Selby wasn't used to talking to anyone, just the occasional monosyllabic answer for her parents.

And yesterday she had been engaged in countless philosophical and literary discussions with Dan, as well as debating life-and-death principles of morality with Hamlet, and even Ophelia. It would be such a relief to sit at the back of a classroom and be ignored.

Mum and Dad were already down in the bookstore when Selby emerged for breakfast. She ate alone, packed her lunch and headed down, turning to call out a perfunctory goodbye as she stepped out through the front door of the shop. Whereupon she slammed into someone and stumbled backwards, landing on her butt.

'Good morning, fair Selby,' said Hamlet as he held out his hand to help her up. 'Falling at my feet already. Has regard for me o'er-powered thee at last?'

'What are you doing here?' asked Selby.

Dan was standing next to him, looking irritated. They were both dressed in hi-vis work shirts. Dan was already dusty. They looked like they'd come straight from the building site.

'I tried taking him to work with me,' said Dan. 'It didn't work out.'

'What happened?' asked Selby.

Dan glanced at Hamlet. 'He got in an argument with a carpenter. The carpenter tried to punch him and Hamlet tried to attack him with a sword. Of course, he didn't have a sword, I made him leave that at home, so he attacked him with a claw hammer instead. The carpenter threatened to call the cops if he didn't leave the site.'

'What were you arguing about?' Selby asked Hamlet. 'It must have been pretty bad if it seemed like a good idea to attack a man with a work tool?'

'He questioned my honour,' said Hamlet.

Selby turned to Dan for an explanation.

'The carpenter teased him for talking like a girl,' said Dan.

'Girls don't talk like that,' said Selby, pointing at Hamlet.

'I know,' said Dan. 'The carpenter isn't the greatest wit. He didn't mean any harm – they always tease new people on a job site. On my first day, they sent me to Bunnings to buy a left-handed screwdriver.'

'Surely you didn't fall for that one,' said Selby.

'Of course not,' said Dan. 'My dad is an electrician.

I grew up holding screwdrivers for him. I went to the bookshop and read for half an hour, then let them laugh at me when I got back. That's how you fit in, by going along with the joke.'

'I'm guessing they didn't have going-along-with-a-joke lessons at prince school,' said Selby.

'There is but little value placed on mirth,' said Hamlet, 'except among the fools who trade in it.'

'Apparently not,' agreed Dan.

'Well, what do you expect me to do with him?' asked Selby.

'Can't he work in the store?' asked Dan.

'I don't want to leave him alone with Mum and Dad,' said Selby. 'What if he tries to hit one of them with a hammer?'

'I would never raise a hand against the parents of the woman I love,' said Hamlet.

'Apart from the fact I refuse to accept that you do love me,' said Selby, 'I seriously doubt you know what love is. You did kill the father of your last girl-friend just yesterday.'

'T'was an accident,' said Hamlet. 'And t'was thou who held my arm throughout the doing of it.'

'Take him to school with you,' said Dan.

'What?' said Selby. 'I can't just take a grown man to school.'

'He looks young enough,' said Dan. 'If anyone asks, just say he's a Danish exchange student. I bet no-one will even ask, though.'

'That's a terrible idea,' said Selby.

'Well, he can't come back to the site with me,' said Dan, backing away towards his van. 'And I've got to get back. It's going to rain this afternoon. We've got to get the wiring done before then.'

'Dan, no, wait!' protested Selby. But Dan had already jumped into the driver's seat of his van. 'Good luck,' he called out the window as he sped away.

'Coward,' muttered Selby.

'What now?' asked Hamlet.

'I guess you're going to come with me,' said Selby. 'If you think medieval Denmark was full of conflict and treachery, wait 'til you see a modern high school.'

'Should I fetch forth my sword?' asked Hamlet.

'Probably not,' said Selby. 'Someone might pull a gun on you.'

'A cannon?' asked Hamlet. 'Thou school has such weaponry?'

'I don't think so,' said Selby. 'But who knows what

they get up to in metal work. The teacher is pretty eccentric. It wouldn't surprise me.'

So Selby and Hamlet set out to school together.

Selby was embarrassed when she walked into her first period English lesson with Hamlet in tow. It turns out, she needn't have been. Everyone ignored her. Of course, they always had ignored her. Acknowledging her would have diminished their own social standing. The fact that she brought a tall, good-looking man to their class was clearly a desperate bid for attention, which they were not going to pander to by asking questions. Selby found two seats at the back for her and Hamlet.

'What lecture are we attending?' he asked.

'English,' said Selby.

'Excellent! Art thou studying a text I may have read?' asked Hamlet.

'In a way, yes,' said Selby. 'We're studying a play called *Hamlet*.'

'Really?' said Hamlet. 'I have never heard of this work.'

'Yes,' agreed Selby. 'You sort of inspired it.'

133

'The English have written a play about me?' asked Hamlet.

'Basically, yes,' said Selby.

'Then, in truth, I shall enjoy this lesson,' said Hamlet. 'In this play, I hope I will find myself to be an excellent teacher.'

'That's a good idea,' said Selby. 'You just listen and take it all in. It's probably best if you don't actively participate in the lesson. Because you're a visitor.'

A harried Ms Karim entered carrying a stack of papers. 'Right, settle down,' she said. 'I hope you all did your reading last night.'

The class groaned.

'But it's so boring, miss,' complained Ben.

'Yeah,' agreed Simon, his friend.

'It's full of murder and ghosts,' said Ms Karim. 'I don't see how you can find that boring.'

'Because it's so hard to understand,' said Michelle, a girl who much preferred science. 'It's all in old English.'

'It's not,' said Ms Karim. 'Old English is from a specific period. This isn't even Middle English. Shakespeare uses Early Modern English. We'll cover

Middle English next semester when we read Chaucer. That is much more challenging.'

'Can't we get a translation?' asked Ben.

'Or watch the movie?' said Simon.

Lots of people started calling out and agreeing with that one.

'No,' said Ms Karim. 'Hamlet's struggles are universal themes that you can all learn from. The language is challenging, but you don't come here to be spoon-fed intellectual baby food. You are here to learn. You need to attempt to actively engage. You need to try. It isn't meant to be easy.'

'Well, I did the reading,' said Isla, 'and I didn't like it because Hamlet is such a dick.'

The class sniggered.

'What did she say?' asked Hamlet.

'Shhh,' said Selby. 'You're just observing, remember.'

'If Hamlet just got to the point, it would all be over so much sooner,' said Isla.

'I just wish he'd make up his mind,' said Olivia. 'It's like taking my nan to the drive thru at McDonalds. I swear she takes ten times longer than she needs to just because she enjoys driving everyone nuts.'

'And he's mean to his girlfriend,' said Isla.

'And his mum,' said Olivia. 'If I spoke to my mum that way, I'd get my wifi cut off.'

'Well, his mum was a tart,' said Ben.

'How dare you!' roared Hamlet, leaping to his feet.

'Don't!' cried Selby. She leapt up and tried to stop Hamlet, but he brushed past her.

'I'll not suffer the ignorance of such fools!' declared Hamlet. He reached for his belt as if to draw his sword, forgetting he was not carrying one. Instead, he picked up the nearest thing to hand – Selby's homework folder – and threatened Ben with it. 'Take back your vile words.'

'Who on earth are you?' demanded Ms Karim.

'I am the teacher who shall school this pup in manners,' said Hamlet. 'If this fledgling scoundrel does not beg my pardon, as a gentleman should, he shall soon beg for his life!'

'You're not a teacher here,' said Ms Karim. 'Who gave you permission to come to this classroom?'

'He's with me, miss,' said Selby. 'He's a . . . Danish exchange student. He knows all about *Hamlet*. He's . . . um . . . a Hamlet impersonator where he comes from. I thought he could help us understand the novel.'

'You can't just bring guests to class,' said Ms Karim.

'Hah! This fits no definition of a class,' said Hamlet. ''Tis a room indeed. I spy four walls and a ceiling above them. But a class should be a room wherein students learn, and mine eyes see no evidence of this amongst this pimply pack of wastrels.'

'I think you'd better leave,' said Ms Karim. 'I'm going to have to report this to the principal, Selby. He will want to talk to you about this. It's not acceptable.'

'How dare you!' accused Hamlet. ''Tis I who shall report you – to the governors of this institution! I'll not stand idly by while you abuse my good lady. Come, Selby, let us leave this place.'

'His *good lady*?' sniggered Mischa.

Selby began packing up her things, trying not to make eye contact with anyone.

'Before you kick him out,' said Isla, holding her hand up. 'Can I ask him a question?' She twisted in her chair to speak to Hamlet. 'What does forsooth mean?'

'Do you not teach them even basic vocabulary?' Hamlet asked Ms Karim scathingly.

'It means in truth,' said Selby. 'They used to say it a lot. I guess because so many weird things happened that weren't believable.'

'Why didn't you just kill your uncle as soon as you found out he had murdered your father?' asked Max.

'Terminating a man's existence is not such an easy task,' said Hamlet. 'The blow of the sword may not take much strength, but the determination of the mind needed is mighty.'

'You were pretty cold about it when you killed Polonius,' said Mary.

'Aye, and I thought it my uncle I was slaying,' said Hamlet. 'That eased the way for my conscience to strike.'

'He was very confused when he saw the ghost,' said Selby, remembering the haunted look on Hamlet's face. 'He couldn't be sure that the ghost was real. That it wasn't a spirit sent by the devil to provoke him into committing an unforgivable crime.'

'But why were you so mean to Ophelia?' asked Wendy.

'Sometimes you have to be cruel to be kind,' said Hamlet. 'She will be better off in a nunnery than by my side. Why, let the strucken deer go weep, the hart ungallèd play, for some must watch while some must sleep, thus runs the world away.'

'Huh?' said Ben.

'Don't listen to him,' said Selby. 'He'll smother you in an avalanche of words. It's simple, really. He lost his temper because he was angry with Ophelia. He knew the king was listening behind the curtain. He felt betrayed that Ophelia was helping them to set him up.'

'Your analysis of the text has improved,' Ms Karim complimented Selby. 'Have you actually read the play at last?'

'Well, no,' admitted Selby. 'But it's not meant to be read. It's meant to be seen performed live. I've seen most of it that way.'

'By hiring a Hamlet impersonator,' said Ben.

The class sniggered.

'No,' said Selby.

Hamlet took her hand and raised it to his lips.

'I am not a man who can be bought and sold for coin,' declared Hamlet. 'I fell in love, as surely as a tree falls under the blade of a sharp axe.'

'Awww,' said several students.

'Ew,' said several others.

'One day, I shall take this lady for my wife,' said Hamlet. 'Her father has agreed to the match. All that remains is to set a date. A week, a day, would be too long to wait for me.'

'Why is this the only thing you're decisive about?' asked Selby.

'My heart beats but one tune,' said Hamlet. 'A love song for you.'

'Miss, I think I'm going to be sick,' said Ben, putting up his hand.

'You're supposed to be setting aside trivial things, remember,' Selby told Hamlet, shaking free her hand.

'You are right,' said Hamlet. 'It would be unforgivable now for me to take a wife when I have sworn a blood oath to avenge my father.'

'That's the excuse all the boys use,' said Deidre. 'I can't go out tonight. I've got to avenge the death of my father.'

Everyone laughed.

'Is she mocking me?' asked Hamlet.

'A little,' said Selby.

'The youths in this place are a most discourteous rabble,' said Hamlet. 'They could all benefit from a thorough thrashing.'

'Arbitrary violence is not the custom here,' explained Selby. 'High school is more about verbal and psychological manipulation and intimidation. I think, once you get used to it, you'd fit in well. You are really good at denouncing people.'

''Tis a princely duty,' said Hamlet.

After English was chemistry. Hamlet did much better in that subject. He was so amazed by the Bunsen burner on their desk, he didn't interrupt the lesson nearly as much. Then middle period was double maths. Hamlet had zero interest in calculus, so he sat quietly and read the books Selby had brought for him.

She thought Hamlet could do some work on himself, so she had grabbed *Who Moved My Cheese?*, *Men Are from Mars, Women Are from Venus* and

Zen and the Art of Motorcycle Maintenance before leaving the store that morning. He pored over them conscientiously, ignoring the class talking around him, except to occasionally mutter to Selby, 'These books have much wisdom' or, 'The tutors at Wittenberg University must read this text'.

At lunchtime, Selby took Hamlet to sit on the far side of the playground, where she shared her sandwich with him.

'The food here tastes so good,' said Hamlet.

Selby had never seen someone enjoy a plain ham-on-white-bread sandwich so much. 'It's probably the artificial colouring and flavour enhancers in the ham.'

'Mmm,' said Hamlet distractedly as he took another bite. He looked around at the playground. 'Why are we sitting in lonely isolation? So far off from all the others? Prithee, tell me, is this a punishment for some misdemeanour you've committed?'

'I always sit alone at lunch,' said Selby.

'Ah, much like myself, you have a preference for the solitude of a good book,' said Hamlet.

'No, I don't read much. I'm a slow reader,' said Selby. 'By the time I figure out the words I lose the sense of what they're saying.'

'So verily you sit alone, doing nothing? Every day?!' asked Hamlet.

'I eat my lunch,' said Selby. 'And I think about stuff.'

'What of those youths o'er yonder, making sport with that ball?' asked Hamlet, pointing out half a dozen kids playing handball.

'I'm not any good at handball,' said Selby. 'My coordination is pathetic. They wouldn't want me to play with them.'

'Can you not pursue the accomplishments of a lady?' asked Hamlet. 'Embroidery and weaving are fine occupations.'

'People don't do that anymore,' said Selby. 'There are machines that do all that sort of thing very quickly and easily.'

'So each day you come to this school, simply waiting for the day when you may stop coming?' asked Hamlet.

'I guess so,' said Selby. 'I hadn't really thought about it that way. School is just something you have to do.'

'In Denmark, school is a luxury for the privileged,' said Hamlet.

'Remember when you said that Denmark was your prison?' said Selby. 'Well that's how school feels for people who aren't good at it. You have to wait out your thirteen years before they let you go.'

13

Something Very Bad

Selby decided to cut class in the afternoon. It was
PE and she didn't think it was a good idea to let
Hamlet get anywhere near the baseball bats, let alone
the javelins. So she took him back to the bookstore.
Selby knew her parents would be angry she'd cut
the last class of the day, but she couldn't dawdle her
way home in case Mrs Tink or some other busybody
spotted her. She needn't have worried. Her parents
didn't even notice that she was home an hour early –
they were too busy finishing off the stocktake.

Selby and Hamlet sat on the stools behind
the counter. Hamlet was reading and eating a
chocolate bar from the jar on the desk. Selby was
doing her biology homework. It was actually very

145

companionable – relaxing even – just hanging out together. Selby was reading about the anatomy of the human ear when the shop bell tinkled. It was Dan.

'My excellent good friend!' exclaimed Hamlet, looking up from his book. 'How dost thou, Dan?'

'All good,' said Dan. He was trying to sound reassuring, but he looked agitated. 'I just need a quick word with Selby.'

'Aye,' said Hamlet. 'I do not much like her conferring with other men, but as her faithful servant I trust that you can be trusted.' Turning to Selby, he continued. 'And trust that my faith will be faithfully upheld.'

'Very clever,' said Selby, patting his hand as she scooted off the stool to go and talk to Dan. She found him at the far back of the store in the children's section.

'What is it?' she asked.

Dan peeked over the top of the shelves to see what Hamlet was doing. He'd gone back to reading his book. He was really enjoying the books from the self-help section.

Dan sat down in the tiny elephant chair put there

to keep young readers happy while their parents browsed. Selby took a seat on a tiny lion.

'We've got to put him back,' whispered Dan.

'What?' said Selby.

'Hamlet,' said Dan. 'He's got to go back into the play.'

'But he's just starting to settle in,' said Selby.

'Really?' said Dan. He leaned back on his elephant seat so he could see around the side of a bookcase.

Hamlet was peering intently at the barcode scanner attached to the register. He accidentally scanned his own face and flinched.

'He's got an enquiring mind,' said Selby.

'You've gotten attached, haven't you?' accused Dan. 'He's not a puppy. You don't get to just keep him because he followed you home from school and he's cute.'

'The whole reason we took him out of the play was to prevent a bloodbath,' said Selby. 'He's not causing any trouble here. He might denounce people more than is polite but, so long as he doesn't get his hands on another sword, he'll be fine.'

'*He* might be fine,' said Dan. 'But his being here is destroying the entire Western canon of literature.'

'The what of what?' said Selby.

'I'll show you,' said Dan. He got up and led Selby over to the classics section. 'Look, here's a copy of *Hamlet*.' Dan picked up the play and showed Selby the cover.

'So?' said Selby.

'Look inside,' said Dan. He started flicking through. Everything looked normal.

'What am I looking at?' asked Selby.

'Nothing yet,' said Dan. 'These are the first two acts. But here . . .' Dan stopped when the pages suddenly went blank. 'This is where we took him out of the play. From this point on, the rest of the play is blank.'

Selby took the book out of Dan's hands and had a look for herself. It was weird. The first half was a perfectly normal book. The second half was entirely blank, except for the page numbers at the bottom.

Dan picked up another copy from the shelf and showed it to her. 'They're all the same.'

'Well, that's a shame,' said Selby. 'But it's worth it. To save – what was it? Eight lives?'

'Eight fictional lives,' said Dan.

'They were real in that world,' argued Selby.

'It gets worse,' said Dan. 'Because *Hamlet* is a pivotal work in the evolution of English literature.'

'Huh?' said Selby.

'That one play influenced so many other books and plays,' said Dan. He grabbed another book from the shelf. 'You've heard of *Great Expectations* by Charles Dickens?'

'Yeah, of course,' said Selby. 'It's a classic. There's a TV version.'

Dan rolled his eyes, 'Yes, well there was, but there probably isn't now. Look at this.'

He flicked through the book – it was entirely empty. 'Because Hamlet has gone, so has *Great Expectations*. It was inspired by *Hamlet*. And it doesn't end there. *Hamlet* influenced Hermin Melville, so that's *Moby Dick* gone. And William Faulkner, who wrote *The Sound and the Fury*, Adolph Huxley and *Brave New World*.

'That's half the classics section!' said Selby. She may not have read them, but you can't grow up in a bookshop and not know those books.

'Exactly,' said Dan. 'And once all those books have gone, then so have all the books they influenced. It's like a giant sinkhole has opened up in the history of literature and books are just disappearing into oblivion.'

'Okay, that's bad,' said Selby.

'Then there are all the words and expressions invented by Shakespeare and first used in Hamlet. "To thine own self be true", "neither a borrower nor a lender be", "to sleep, perchance to dream", "brevity is the soul of wit", "the lady doth protest too much", "conscience doth make cowards of us all", "I must be cruel only to be kind". That's all gone.'

'But still,' said Selby. 'The deaths.'

'They are fictional,' said Dan. 'We can't confuse real life and fantasy.'

'This from the guy who plays Dungeons and Dragons every weekend,' said Selby.

'We have to let their story play out,' said Dan, 'because, in the world of books, *Hamlet* is one of the most important stories ever told. And books are important. The advance of ideas and literary expression is how civilisation evolves. To keep Hamlet here would be devolutionary!'

'Oh, please. Melodramatic much?' said Selby.

'Yes, yes I am!' said Dan. 'Because you don't get it. You live here in a building surrounded by books, but you can't see how important they are. You can't see the wood for the trees. Books are time capsules of ideas. They are how knowledge and wisdom and art are transferred through time. They are important. We can't vandalise that.'

Selby stared at the floor, trying to wrap her mind around all this. It was a lot. She could see that Dan was right. But she also knew, instinctively, that it was utterly wrong to allow people to just die. She didn't buy Dan's argument that they were fictional so it was okay. It didn't feel okay.

She looked across at Hamlet, talking to her mother. Her mother was laughing, but she looked a little nervous too. Hamlet was no doubt saying something clever with three different veiled meanings. Apart from anything else, if she put him back in the play, she would miss him.

Selby had been such a pale excuse for a human being. Like a watercolour painting, transparent in places, in others no colour there at all. She'd gone unnoticed for so long – it had been fun to hang out with someone utterly brash, and confident and even loudly abusive. She couldn't conceive of behaving that way herself, but it had been fun to watch someone else doing it. Hamlet was so flawed. And his ideas were totally messed up. But she admired his bravery.

Even his indecision and what he considered his own cowardice, it was really just a determination to be sure.

She had to do the right thing, but she would do it on her own terms.

'I'll put him back,' said Selby. 'But I'm not going to let them all die. I'll do it, but only if I can get Ophelia out first.'

'That would change the narrative,' said Dan.

'Good!' said Selby. 'The narrative sucks.'

Dan winced.

'Did you just wince because I said "sucks", or because I criticised Shakespeare's plotting?' asked Selby.

'A little bit of both,' said Dan.

'Look, taking Ophelia out wouldn't change it much,' said Selby. 'She doesn't directly influence any of the plot once she's dead. So if, instead of dying, she disappeared – then it wouldn't affect the rest of the plot at all.'

'I suppose so,' said Dan, running the rest of the play through in his mind. 'That should work. It would be easy enough for her to simply disappear down by the river, instead of drowning.'

'Then that's what we'll do,' said Selby. 'I'll go back in and get Ophelia out. You mind Hamlet. Then once she's out, he can go back in and the story can play out.'

'Okay,' said Dan. He took out the copy of *Hamlet* and found the right page for her. He glanced at the text himself, then looked up at Selby. 'Be careful. At this point where you're going back into in the play – it's very sad. Ophelia is devasted by her father's death.'

He held out the book to Selby. She knew this was going to be hard, but there was no avoiding it. Selby took it and started reading out loud, but soon, the voice in her ears was Ophelia's . . .

OPHELIA   *I hope all will be well.*
We must be patient,
but I cannot choose but weep,
to think they would lay him i'th'
cold ground.
My brother shall know of it,
and so I thank you for your good
counsel.
Come, my coach.
Good night, ladies, good night,
sweet ladies,
good night, good night.

153

14

Helping Ophelia

Selby tumbled out through the wall and landed with a thump in the gardens of Castle Elsinore. She hadn't been out here before. It was beautiful. She was surrounded by ornamental flower beds and espaliered fruit trees, all in blossom, lining the wall she had just fallen through. A movement caught her eye. It was Ophelia. She was carrying a basket as she disappeared into the woods beyond the formal gardens. Selby hurried after her.

Selby wasn't too worried about losing sight of Ophelia, because she could hear her singing. It was eerie – the singing of someone so devastated they had emotionally checked out. Selby walked deeper and deeper into the forest, following the sound.

The undergrowth was thick. She only caught occasional glimpses of Ophelia's pale pink dress as she moved through the forest.

The path was winding downwards. Pretty soon, Selby could hear the babble of moving water. They were getting close to the river. Selby hurried her pace. She wanted to get to the riverbank before Ophelia could do anything. The undergrowth was lush and thicker here. She couldn't see Ophelia up ahead at all. She couldn't hear the singing either. It was making Selby nervous.

Suddenly – there was a loud *SPLASH*!

Selby knew immediately – this was bad. Adrenalin kicked in. She gave up following the path and crashed straight through the undergrowth towards the sound of the river.

As she broke through, Selby almost stumbled into the water where the bank dropped away steeply. It was a large, fast-moving river. Selby saw Ophelia's basket float past. Flowers were scattered on the top of the water. The blooms were just starting to become waterlogged and sink. It was a chilling sight. Selby looked upstream along the bank. She could see Ophelia fifty metres away. The distraught girl was wading out into the water. Her long skirt was already totally drenched. Ophelia was reaching for a flower that hung from a branch above.

'Stop!' cried Selby.

Ophelia didn't seem to hear her.

Selby ran up the bank, but she slipped on the mud and fell into the river. The water was only a couple of feet deep. Selby pulled herself up and started to wade out to Ophelia.

'Stop!' Selby yelled again.

But Ophelia was wading in deeper. She was up to her chest.

Selby realised she was not going to get there before Ophelia got caught in the current, but she could also see that the current would bring Ophelia towards her. So instead of continuing up the bank, Selby waded out into the deeper water to be ready to intercept her.

Ophelia suddenly lost her footing and was pulled into the current. She disappeared below the water for one heart-stopping moment before her head bobbed up and she gasped for breath, but the river had caught hold of her and she went under again.

Selby desperately waded in deeper, praying she was far enough out to catch Ophelia as she came towards her. If she couldn't catch hold of her, Ophelia would be swept away downstream. The current was strong. It was a struggle to stay upright and Selby was only waist deep.

All the things Selby had ever learned in water rescue at school started rattling through her mind. *Don't let a drowning person grab you. Grab them from behind or they'll pull you under and you'll both drown.*

Ophelia was drawing towards her swiftly. The eddies of the water kept pulling her under. Selby reached out. But she wasn't going to catch her. She wasn't out far enough. Selby pushed off from the bottom of the river and swam out deeper. She was out of her depth and into the current herself. Selby stretched right out.

She saw Ophelia's face under the water. Her eyes were open. She was still alive. But she made no attempt to save herself. Selby grabbed hold of Ophelia's dress by the shoulder, then rolled onto her own back, pulling Ophelia up on top of her chest and drawing her face up above the water. Ophelia instinctively gasped for breath. Selby slid her arm under Ophelia's armpits and lay back to get as buoyant as possible before she started to swim side-stroke towards to the bank.

It was really hard. Ophelia didn't help at all, and they were both fully clothed. Ophelia's long dress was like an anchor. The water pulled at it, making it hard for Selby to hold on to her. But Selby's swimming instruction was in her mind. *Don't swim against the current. Swim across it.* It was painfully slow, and exhausting, but Selby knew they were making progress towards the bank even as they swept further and further downstream. Gradually, they were edging closer to dry land.

After what felt like an age, Selby realised she was able to stand up. Ophelia was almost swept out of her arms by the current when she did. But she hung on, and slowly dragged Ophelia to the bank. When Selby finally pulled them both up on to the shore they were totally bedraggled, mud-smeared and drenched.

'Are you okay?' asked Selby.

'My father is dead,' muttered Ophelia.

'I know,' said Selby. 'I'm so sorry.'

'Go to thy deathbed,' Ophelia half sang, 'he never will come again.' In her high-pitched, childlike voice, it sounded like a nursery rhyme from a nightmare. But the devastation in Ophelia's face was too real to trivialise.

'I know you feel terrible now,' said Selby. 'I know you are in a lot of pain, and you can't imagine ever feeling better. But I promise you, you will.'

Ophelia didn't say anything. She just stared back with vacant eyes. Selby got the sense she was disappointed to have been rescued. She felt terrible for this poor girl, but there was no doubt in her mind that she had done the right thing.

'Now let's just get through the next ten minutes,' said Selby. Ophelia obviously wasn't capable of having a conversation. That was okay. Selby would talk for both of them. It was as much for her own benefit – she needed to reassure herself. 'We are going to get up and walk back to where you went into the river. From there, I'm going to find my way back to the portal. Then I'm going to find someone who can help you. All you have to do is come with me on a walk for ten minutes. I'm going to take you somewhere where there will be help.'

'He is gone, he is gone,' mumbled Ophelia. 'And we cast away moan, God-a-mercy on his soul.'

'I know,' said Selby. 'It's terrible. But you can do this. Just walk with me a little way.'

Selby helped Ophelia up. Ophelia was actually steadier on her legs than Selby was herself, because she hadn't done any swimming. Selby took Ophelia by the arm and started walking with her up the riverbank.

'And in his grave rained many a tear,' said Ophelia. 'Fare you well, my dove.'

Selby did not know what to say to this poor, distraught girl, but she felt she had to say something. 'When my friend Dan's mum died, he was very sad,' said Selby. 'I can't imagine what he felt. But he used to come to the bookstore every day and look at books. He'd pick one out and go home and read it. Then be back the next day for another book. I think they were a comfort to him. A book can be a way of taking a holiday from yourself, stepping into someone else's shoes. At least that's what they say. I don't read much myself. I find it hard to focus on the words. But I like stories. Where I come from, we have stories acted out for us, like the plays you watch, only ours are in these boxes we have in our homes called televisions.'

Ophelia glanced at her.

'Anyway, stories are comforting when you are sad,' said Selby. 'I know a place with lots of books. You might like it. Also, we have counsellors and doctors who can help people who are so sad that their minds get confused. Let me help you. Things will get better eventually. I promise.'

15

Criss Cross

G etting Ophelia all the way back to the castle was not easy and it took some time, but people stayed out of their way. Anyone they came across veered away at the sight of Ophelia. It was almost as if they feared grief and mental illness like it was a contagious disease. When they got back to the portal, Selby carefully reached out to check if she could still pass through. The wall felt like it was buzzing or vibrating.

'Come on,' said Selby. She wrapped her arm Ophelia's shoulders and lead her towards the garden wall where Selby had arrived only an hour earlier.

Ophelia understandably baulked at walking straight into brickwork.

'It's okay,' Selby assured her. 'Close your eyes. Trust me. I'm taking you somewhere better.'

Ophelia did as she was told. She always did. Being so obedient was a big part of her problem. In this case, hopefully, it actually would be for her own best interest. Ophelia closed her eyes and stepped forward as Selby guided her, and soon they were passing through the garden wall and falling into the wind of words . . .

CLAUDIUS   *Revenge should have no bounds.*
But, good Laertes,
Will you do this, keep close within
your chamber.
Hamlet, returned, shall know you
are come home . . .

Moments later, Selby found herself collapsing on the floor of the bookstore. Dan wrapped her shoulders in a towel. She looked up. He really was unreasonably tall.

'You thought to get towels?' she said, rolling over and sitting up.

'I figured you'd both be wet,' said Dan.

Selby saw that he had already wrapped Ophelia in a big fluffy bathrobe. She looked so young here, out of her natural context. Ophelia was staring at Dan in wonder.

'You sent for me?' she asked.

'No. Now don't you get any ideas,' said Selby firmly. 'Dan cannot marry you. Because . . .'

She looked at Dan to see if he could think of a good excuse.

'Because . . . I am already pledged to another,' said Dan.

'Okay, I guess that will work,' said Selby. She turned to Ophelia, 'Look I don't think you're in a good headspace to get into another relationship right now. Have you heard about rebound relationships?'

'No,' said Ophelia.

'Well that's what Dan would be,' said Selby. 'He seems really good because he's tall and his face is all symmetrical and all that superficial stuff girls go for. But, really, you're mainly attracted to him because he's not Hamlet.'

'I do protest these harsh words!' said Hamlet, coming over to see what was going on. He was surprised to see his ex-girlfriend. 'Ophelia! Prithee tell me, what devilry brings her hither?'

'You, behave!' Selby snapped at Hamlet. 'I'm only speaking the truth. After time with you, any guy who doesn't berate her and tell her to become a nun is going to look pretty good.'

'She is really going to struggle here in the modern world,' said Dan.

'I agree,' said Selby. 'Can we put her into another book? Somewhere where men are more polite. She's always been controlled by the men in her life – her father, her brother and Hamlet. I don't think she needs the social workers and the counsellors we have here now. I think it would be good for her to spend some time with girls her own age.'

'I've got an idea,' said Dan.

'What?' said Selby.

'*Pride and Prejudice*,' said Dan.

'The book?' asked Selby.

'Yes,' said Dan. 'It's full of young women, loving sisters. If we put in another one, no-one will notice.'

'You reckon?' asked Selby.

'Sure,' said Dan. 'A couple of them are hysterical and crazy for men in uniform. Ophelia will fit in.

And the older sisters Elizabeth and Jane are sensible and kind. They'll look after her.'

'But would they agree to it?' asked Selby.

'Elizabeth will,' said Dan. 'She's got a good sense of humour.'

'I guess it's no crazier than leaving her here,' said Selby. 'Let's do it.'

Dan found a copy of *Pride and Prejudice* on the shelf and handed it to Selby to read.

'Read it out loud,' urged Dan.

'Will it work with another book?' asked Selby, suddenly hit with a wave of self-doubt.

'There's one way to find out,' said Dan.

Selby looked down at the first page of the first chapter and started reading the words out loud. She reached out without looking and grabbed Dan's hand. He took hold of Ophelia's. They all started to tumble forward into the words.

> *It is a truth universally acknowledged,*
> *that a single man in possession of a good fortune,*
> *must be in want of a wife.*
> *However little known the feelings or views*
> *of such a man may be*

on his first entering a neighbourhood,
this truth is so well fixed in the minds of the
surrounding families,
that he is . . .

Selby felt herself tumbling over and over until suddenly – she was lying flat on her back in the long grass, looking up at a bright blue sky. There were wildflowers amongst the grass – primroses and daisies. She could hear bees buzzing about and, some distance off, a cow lowing.

Selby sat up. She was in the middle of a field. Across the valley was a beautiful patchwork of hedge lined fields, neatly framed against the rolling hills. The sun was starting to dip in the sky. It was late afternoon. The countryside felt drowsy with the warm sunshine. A patch of daffodils caught Selby's eye. She didn't think she had ever seen anything so yellow. It was as if the sunshine had been captured and transformed into a flower.

'Run!' cried Dan.

Selby turned to see Dan sprinting towards her, carrying Ophelia in his arms. Selby was confused for one moment, until she saw why Dan was running.

There was an angry bull galloping at full speed towards him. Selby leapt up and took off running too. The three of them only just got to the field's gate in time to throw themselves over before the bull angrily smashed his forehead into the timberwork.

'That was a close call,' said Dan.

'After all the sword play and death threats,' said Selby. 'It would be very anti-climactic to be killed by a cow.'

'You saved me,' Ophelia said to Dan. She didn't seem particularly grateful, more confused.

'I promised you things were going to get better,' Selby told her. 'Hopefully that's the last traumatic event for you for a while.'

'Come on,' said Dan. 'That must be Longbourn.' He pointed to a large and lovely house on the far side of the valley. 'Let's go and introduce ourselves.'

They were walking up the driveway to the main house when, from a side path, a woman climbed over a stile. When she looked up, she was surprised to see them.

'Good day,' said the young woman politely, which was gracious of her because Selby and Ophelia must have looked strange to her in their clothing, and Dan must have been the first person of colour she had ever seen. She probably assumed they were gypsies.

'Are you Miss Bennet?' asked Dan.

'Miss *Elizabeth* Bennet, sir, although I am quite sure we have not been introduced,' said Elizabeth. Selby looked at her closely. Elizabeth was pretty, except for her eyes – they were something more – beautiful and intelligent, with humour behind them. 'Who, pray tell, are you?'

'Well, this is going to sound crazy,' said Selby. 'But we are time travellers from the future.'

'Except for her,' said Dan, pointing at Ophelia. 'She's from the past.'

'We need help,' said Selby. 'This girl's father has recently died. And she has been very badly treated.' Ophelia was not listening. She had bent down to pick wildflowers near her feet. 'She has no-one to look after her. No-one with her best interests at heart.'

Elizabeth frowned. 'You had better come in and have a cup of tea, so we can hear all about it.'

Half an hour later, Selby, Dan and Ophelia were sitting in the drawing room at Longbourn, having explained the situation to Elizabeth and Jane Bennet over a cup of tea.

'The poor girl,' said Jane. 'We must help her.'

'Yes, she must stay here with us,' agreed Elizabeth. 'She can't be as foolish as Lydia, or indeed Mary. She won't be any trouble.'

'But what shall we tell the neighbours?' asked Jane.

'We'll simply say she is a second cousin, come to visit,' said Elizabeth. 'Dear Mama has so many cousins that will be very easy to believe.'

'Yes, I suppose so,' agreed Jane. 'But Ophelia is such an unusual name.'

'You could give her a new name,' suggested Selby. 'It might be nice for her to have a fresh start with a new identity.'

'Is there a name you like the sound of, my dear?' Jane asked kindly.

Ophelia looked up. She was confused by the question.

'If we are to give you a new name,' pressed Jane, 'is there one in particular that you like?'

'Katherine,' said Ophelia. 'T'was my mother's name.'

'And it is a lovely one,' said Elizabeth. 'It will suit you very well. We'll tell everyone you're Katherine, Kitty for short. And that you've come for a long stay.'

'That should work splendidly,' said Jane.

'Your parents won't mind?' asked Dan.

'Mama will be glad of another girl to fuss over,' said Elizabeth. 'And Papa will be persuaded. Five silly girls will be much the same as four to him.'

'I'm to live here, in this magnificent house?' asked Ophelia.

'If you want to,' said Selby. 'It's not safe for you to go home now your father is gone. Do you like it here?'

'Yes,' said Ophelia, looking out at the spring garden. 'I like the flowers.'

And so, it was decided. Selby and Dan left Ophelia in the chronicles of the Bennet family. Ophelia was a little bit weepy when she realised they were leaving her, but then Lydia, the youngest Bennet sister, bustled in with all the gossip from the village. She started showing her new 'cousin' the ribbons she had bought to dress her hat and Ophelia was soon distracted.

'We should go,' said Dan.

'It's like leaving a child at preschool for the first time,' said Selby. 'You wait until they're distracted then sneak away. Do you think she'll be okay?'

'She'll be better off,' said Dan. 'If you hadn't gone back for her, she'd be dead.'

It was a sobering thought. Ophelia didn't look happy or even particularly stable, but she was alive. She had a chance.

Selby and Dan walked back across the valley to where they had arrived. The bull was distracted by his dinner at the far side of the field. It was easy to find the exact spot because the wild flowers were still crushed where they had landed.

Dan held out a copy of *Pride and Prejudice* to her. 'Read us home.'

Selby looked at the page and started to read . . .

> *You are too sensible a girl, Lizzy,*
> *to fall in love merely because you are warned*
> *against it;*
> *and, therefore, I am not afraid of speaking*
> *openly.*
> *Seriously I would have you be on your*
> *guard . . .*

Selby and Dan were soon flat on their backs in the bookstore again.

'What is it with you two and lying on the floor?' demanded Mum. 'Is there something I need to know? Do you have an inner-ear infection? Are you suffering from low blood pressure?'

'We were just reading,' said Selby, getting to her feet.

'That's almost as unnerving,' said Mum.

'You wanted me to read more,' said Selby.

'I didn't know it was going to overpower you and you'd lose the ability to stand,' said Mum. She turned on Dan and glowered at him suspiciously. 'I certainly expected better from you.'

'Sorry, Mrs Michaels,' said Dan.

'Humpf,' said Mum as she continued to the back of the shop.

'We did the right thing, didn't we?' Selby asked Dan. 'I feel like I just abandoned a puppy on someone's doorstep.'

'Let's see . . .' said Dan. He opened *Pride and Prejudice*. '. . . If it worked, she should be in here now.' He started flicking through the pages. 'Look, there she is!' Dan pointed to the name Kitty on the page.

'Wow, it actually worked,' said Selby. Looking over Dan's shoulder she could see the name Kitty right there in the text.

> *. . . they quickly perceived, in token of the coachman's punctuality, both Kitty and Lydia looking out of a dining room upstairs. These two girls had been above an hour in the place, happily employed in visiting an opposite milliner, watching the sentinel on guard, and dressing a salad and cucumber.*

'You see, she's okay,' said Dan.

'Good for her,' said Selby. 'There are no deadly sword fights in this book, are there?'

'You really should read it for yourself,' said Dan.

'Oh, come on,' said Selby. 'I'm just asking if she ends okay.'

'Well, the book is mainly about getting married,' said Dan as he flicked through the final chapters. 'Lydia ends up with a cad, but she does get married. And Kitty . . . Here we go . . .' Dan read it aloud himself.

*Kitty, to her very material advantage, spent
the chief of her time with her two elder sisters.
In society so superior to what she had generally
known, her improvement was great.*

'I'm glad she got a happy ending,' said Selby.

'She did have a rotten character arc in *Hamlet*,'
agreed Dan.

'Speaking of such,' said Selby. 'I'd better put him
back.'

16

Back Again

Dan got out their now very beaten up copy of *Hamlet* and started flicking through the pages.

'What point in the play should I be taking him back to?' asked Selby.

'The next big scene is the one with the grave digger,' said Dan. 'That's the famous speech where Hamlet talks to the skull. You know – "Alas, poor Yorick" – that bit.'

'So we go back to there?' said Selby.

'No, that scene can't happen now,' said Dan. 'That whole scene takes place in the churchyard when Hamlet comes across two gravediggers, who are digging a grave for Ophelia. But you've saved her, so that plot point has been erased.'

'I'm surprised you're not upset,' said Selby. 'If I've just wiped out a famous Shakespearean speech.'

Dan shrugged. 'Maybe there will be a different, better speech now. This plot is better. All good writers need a good editor.'

'So when I take Hamlet back,' said Selby. 'What will happen?'

'There will be a fencing match between Hamlet and Ophelia's brother, Laertes,' said Dan. 'But the whole thing is a set-up. It isn't really a sporting match. Laertes' blade is poisoned. And just in case that doesn't work, the king also poisons Hamlet's wine. It's a duel to the death. The king talks Laertes into it so he can get revenge.'

'But if Ophelia hasn't died,' said Selby. 'There's no need for a duel.'

'The duel was never about her,' said Dan. 'It's about Polonius.'

'Oh yes, their dad,' said Selby. 'That feels so long ago.' She was getting tired and finding it hard to keep up.

'The duel is to avenge his death,' said Dan. 'Ophelia is never mentioned at the fight, so it should still take place.'

'And whose death am I trying to prevent this time?' asked Selby.

'All of them,' said Dan. 'Hamlet and Laertes both die. So do the queen and king.'

'Wow, that's quite a duel,' said Selby.

'Shakespeare had a thing with ending stories that way,' said Dan. 'Sometimes, all the characters live happily ever after. Sometimes, they all die.'

'Okay, I'll take Hamlet back,' said Selby. 'But first, I've got an idea from my biology homework that might solve a lot of this conflict. I need to find a book.'

'What book?' asked Dan.

'Not in your line,' said Selby. 'From the non-fiction section. Do you think this trick of reading my way into a book would work with non-fiction as well?'

'I don't know,' said Dan. 'It's so weird. I wouldn't think so. I think it's the story that has the magic.'

'I'll just have to take the book then,' said Selby.

She disappeared down into the back of the store, then emerged a few moments later carrying a large tome. 'Come on, your highness,' she called out to Hamlet, who was sitting on the stool behind the counter, reading. 'I've got to take you back to Denmark.'

'To my prison?' said Hamlet.

'No need to be such a Nelly Negative,' said Selby, grabbing his hand and pulling him to his feet. 'You know you have duties to attend to there.'

'Aye, forsooth, it is my duty to murder mine uncle,' said Hamlet.

'Yes, there's that,' said Selby. 'But I was thinking more of the fact that you are heir to the kingdom of Denmark. You might spare a thought for the entire country of people looking to you for leadership.'

Hamlet sighed. 'Aye, 'tis so. From my mother's womb I came forth, already with the yoke of duty heavy upon my shoulders.'

'You whinge too much,' said Selby.

'I know not this word you speak,' said Hamlet.

'Probably for the best,' said Dan, handing Selby the copy of *Hamlet*. 'Don't pick a fight with him now,' Dan told Selby. He pointed to a passage. 'Start reading here.'

Selby found the spot, concentrated for a second and began to read. She and Hamlet were soon drawn forward, down into the text . . .

HAMLET *Since no man of aught he leaves*
knows,
what is't to leave betimes? Let be.

A table prepared, with flagons of wine on it.
Trumpets, drums and officers with cushions.

Selby and Hamlet materialised back in the great
hall of the castle, but they were hidden behind a
curtain. Selby tucked the play in the pocket of her
jacket.

'Why do all this?' asked Hamlet.

'What?' said Selby.

'Why are you helping me and Ophelia, and my
mother?' asked Hamlet. 'You have your own life brim
full of drama and intrigue. Why forsake your world
and undertake so much for mine?'

Selby was surprised at such a genuine and simple
question. Hamlet usually spoke in riddles. 'Because
you need help,' she said simply.

'True,' said Hamlet. 'But what do you want in
return?'

'To go home,' said Selby. 'Without a guilty
conscience.'

'We all of us are sinners,' said Hamlet.

'Yes, but that is no excuse to do less than your best,' said Selby.

You would think, having watched so many day-time soap operas, that Selby would be able to foresee what was about to happen. But it was dark behind the curtain and she was preoccupied with how she was going to handle the duel, so when Hamlet started to lean towards her, it just didn't occur to Selby that he was going to kiss her. When his lips pressed to hers, she was shocked. She was extra especially shocked when he wrapped his arms around her and pulled her against his chest. Selby pushed herself away.

'What are you doing?' said Selby. 'Apart from the fact that you are way too old for me. This is so not the time.'

'Once more, you give me sage counsel,' said Hamlet. He reached out with a finger and touched her cheek. 'Witches and fools are the only truthtellers to princes and kings.'

'You would be better off if you didn't label everyone,' said Selby. 'I'm not a witch or a fool. I'm just a girl.'

'And yet to be thus is to be all three,' said Hamlet.

'Okay, enough with the entrenched sixteenth century misogyny,' said Selby. 'You've got quite a talent for picking fights, you know?'

Hamlet heard the sound of furniture being moved. He looked around the edge of the curtain. 'What's this?' asked Hamlet.

Servants were bustling about, drawing the furniture to the sides of the room and placing two thrones at one end. The king and queen entered with Laertes and other courtiers.

'Your uncle has set up a fencing match between you and Laertes,' explained Selby. 'He's bet lots of horses and weapons on it.'

'Which one of us has he bet on?' asked Hamlet.

'Apparently, you,' said Selby as she consulted her copy of the play.

'I see,' said Hamlet, 'I embrace it freely, and will this brother's wager frankly play.'

'Don't,' urged Selby. 'Nothing is predestined. You don't have to go through with this – not the way it was written.'

But it was too late. Hamlet had stepped out into the room and the king had spotted him. 'Come, Hamlet,' called out the king. 'Come and take this hand from me.' The king grabbed Laertes' hand and held it out to Hamlet. Laertes looked like he'd rather chop his hand off than shake with Hamlet.

'This is bad,' muttered Selby. 'This is really bad.' She started leafing through the play, desperate to find the spot they were up to and to figure out what was about to happen next. The words were swimming before her eyes.

Out in the room, Hamlet broke the moment. He held out his hand to Laertes, Ophelia's brother, Polonius's son, and said, 'Give me your pardon, sir, I've done you wrong.'

Selby was so surprised to hear Hamlet admit he was wrong, she peeked around the edge of the curtain.

'But pardon't as you are a gentleman,' continued Hamlet, 'I am punished with a sore distraction. What I have done, that might your nature, honour and exception roughly awake, I here proclaim was madness. If't be so, Hamlet is of the faction wronged. His madness is poor Hamlet's enemy.'

'Oh, thank goodness he apologised,' Selby whispered to herself.

Laertes did not seem willing to accept the apology. 'I am satisfied in nature,' he said through gritted teeth, 'whose motive in this case should stir me most to my revenge. But in my terms of honour I stand aloof.'

No doubt to stop them killing each other before the fight had a chance to start properly, the king stepped in between.

'Give them the foils, young Osric,' ordered the king, calling out to a courtier who held a collection of fencing blades. 'Come, begin. And you, the judges –' the king glared at the men who would umpire the match – 'bear a wary eye.'

Hamlet and Laertes faced each other and bowed.

'If Hamlet give the first or second hit,' declared the king. 'The king shall drink to Hamlet's better breath!' The king poured out two cups of wine. One for himself and one for Hamlet.

Hamlet and Laertes took guard ready to fight.

'Stop!' cried Selby, running forward to stand between Hamlet and Laertes. 'Stop the fight!'

''Tis not a fight,' said Hamlet. 'But good-natured play. A contest betwixt brothers.'

'You're right,' said Selby. 'It's not a fight. It's murder. Premeditated, accidental and in the heat of passion. Four times over in the next ten minutes if you don't listen to me.'

'Hamlet, school your unruly attendant in the proper manners of court,' ordered the king.

'Let us heed her,' urged Hamlet, 'for she is wise beyond her years. She has opened my mind to many wonderous things, and shown me a world of books most fantastical.'

'Yes, books. That's how I know,' said Selby. 'I've been reading ahead.' She shook her now battered copy of *Hamlet* at them. 'The first person to die at this fight will not be Hamlet, or Laertes. It will be the queen.' Selby pointed at Hamlet's mother. She seemed shocked to suddenly find herself the topic of conversation.

'What, I?' said the queen. 'Am I to take up a blade in my son's defence?'

'No,' said Selby. 'You will drink from that cup.' She indicated the goblet in front of the king that he had set forward for Hamlet. 'The king has put poison in it. Poison intended to kill Hamlet.'

'She is mad,' said the king.

'Mad is a word that has been used a lot since I came here,' said Selby. 'And yet I don't think any of you are mad. Except perhaps for poor Ophelia, and even then, it is not so much mental illness as crushing grief.'

'It seems to me that *you* are mad, young maiden,' accused the king.

'I am,' agreed Selby. 'But not mad in the sense of being insane. I'm mad in the sense that I am angry at you all for being so pig-headed and violent. The only reason you constantly talk of Hamlet as being mad is to discredit him.'

The king had had enough. 'Guards, seize this fishwife who dares to berate a king,' he ordered.

Guards hurried forward to grab Selby, but Hamlet barred their way, 'Stand down,' he counter-ordered.

'If I am mad or lying,' Selby challenged the king, 'then you won't hesitate to drink from Hamlet's cup.'

The king baulked.

'Why do you pause, Uncle?' asked Hamlet. 'Drink. We all know how you love your wine. Drink.'

'It may be poisoned at another's hand,' said the king.

'But it is my cup,' said Hamlet. 'You poured the wine yourself. Drink.'

'I will not,' said the king. 'I know not which tricks this girl is up to.'

'Okay,' said Selby. 'It's probably best you don't drink it anyway, because I don't want your death on my conscience. Let's try something different. How about you all talk through your problems. If you just communicated with each other, and expressed your concerns, you wouldn't be so paranoid and deluded.'

'Ay, she speaks well,' said Hamlet. 'This is the same matter I have read of in this very wise and excellent book of men and women from other planets.' Hamlet took out his copy of *Men Are from Mars, Women Are from Venus* and showed it to the room. 'This text puts forth the discourse that there would be less conflict betwixt the sexes if but woman would let man retreat to his cave. And, in counter measure, man would let woman speak of her woes in his loving embrace. There is much truth here.'

'Thanks, Hamlet,' said Selby. 'That's very true. But it's not the point I was getting at. I suspect that this whole conflict in your family has, at its heart, a big misunderstanding.'

'Explain yourself,' urged Hamlet. 'Surely murder most foul is a simple matter.'

'Well, it's not,' said Selby. 'You think that the king murdered your father by pouring poison in his ear while he was sleeping.'

'What treason is this?' demanded the king, leaping to his feet.

'It is not idle speculation,' said Hamlet. 'Mine own father has come to be in a ghostly form and told me thus.'

'Yes, I saw the ghost say it,' concurred Selby. 'Horatio was there too.'

Horatio nodded. ''Tis so,' he agreed.

'And the accusations of this most worthy ghost were proven true,' accused Hamlet. 'By your own self with your guilty conscience and blustering rage on witnessing the play.'

'Guards, I say, seize this wench at once,' ordered the king again.

But again, Hamlet held up his sword to prevent them.

'Hold your horses.' Selby grabbed Hamlet's sword arm. 'Look, I know you think it's true, Hamlet. But I know that in fact – your uncle did *not* kill your father.'

'What devilry do you speak?' asked Hamlet.

'I believe he did pour poison in your father's ear. But that would not kill him,' said Selby.

'Explain yourself,' ordered Hamlet.

'Your father, the ghost, said he was poisoned with hebenon,' explained Selby. 'But I read up on it in my biology textbook. Hebenon *is* a deadly poison if consumed in a large enough amount, but there is no way you could get a large dose into a man via his ear.'

'What?' said Hamlet.

'Here,' said Selby, taking a big book from her tote bag. 'This is a biology textbook. According to this . . .' Selby showed Hamlet the relevant page. '. . . the volume of the ear canal in an adult man is only two point five cubic centimetres.'

'What is this "centimetre" of which you speak?' asked Hamlet.

'Okay,' said Selby. 'My bad. I forgot you haven't gone metric yet.' Selby looked about for something of relative size that would mean something to Hamlet. She spotted a bowl of nuts and grabbed some. 'Alright, the inside of your ear is tiny. It's about the same size as a hazelnut. Also, the ear canal runs alongside the bone of the skull. Bone is not very absorbent. That means not much liquid can soak in there. Especially because the ear canal is also lined with wax, which also prevents absorption.'

'So my father was not poisoned?' asked Hamlet. He was stunned by this idea. Avenging his father's death had consumed his mind for so long now. It was hard to reorientate his thinking.

'Not fatally, no,' said Selby. 'Even if your father had a ruptured ear drum and all two point five cubic centimetres of poison had drained through his ear, and from there through the Eustachian tube that join the ears to the throat, and then into his digestive system, that amount would not have been enough to kill him.'

'Then of what cause did he die?' asked Hamlet.

'Well, how old was your father?' asked Selby.

'Six and fifty,' said Hamlet.

'Okay, so he was fifty-six,' said Selby. 'That's old for the sixteenth century. Plus, he'd had a long career fighting wars and running a country. That's a stressful job. And he was good at it, which meant lots of feasting, which meant lots of high-fat foods and drinking. His arteries were probably clogged. The small amount of poison could have triggered a heart attack.'

'A what?' asked Hamlet.

'The blood vessels to his heart became blocked,'

190

said Selby, 'from years of calcification. That's like a build-up of gunk you might get in a drain pipe. Only when that pipe is a blood vessel leading into your heart – a build-up becomes deadly.'

'Then my uncle still did kill him?!' said Hamlet.

'Yes, but it puts a different twist on it, doesn't it?' said Selby.

'I will be revenged,' said Hamlet, glaring at his uncle.

'Okay, before you get your revenge,' said Selby, grabbing hold of Hamlet's sword arm again. 'I've got one more thing to say about that. The poison your uncle used is called hebenon. It does not cause death when administered through the ear. But if administered through food or drink, it will cause delusional thinking, mood swings and erratic behaviour.'

'What is your point?' asked Hamlet.

'Think about it,' said Selby. 'Delusional thinking, mood swings, erratic behaviour – does that sound familiar?'

Hamlet still looked baffled.

'Why, 'tis you, Hamlet,' said the queen. 'You have been all these things these past months.'

'I have?' asked Hamlet.

'You just said so yourself to Laertes,' said Selby. 'You said that you are mad, that your madness has made you do these terrible things and that you, more than anyone, are a victim of your own madness.'

'That is what you did say,' agreed Laertes.

'Your behaviour has been totally out of character,' said Selby. 'Everyone says you're a smart, academic guy and you're beloved by the people of Denmark. But all I've seen, since I've been here, is you been behaving terribly.'

'Not so very bad, surely,' said Hamlet. ''Tis is but a tempest of the mind.'

'Oh no,' said Selby. 'You've been dreadful. You've been horrible to your girlfriend, really rude and rough with your mother and sociopathically unconcerned about the fate of your university friends. I think someone has been systematically poisoning you, which has been driving you literally mad, and that has been why your mind is so tortured.'

Hamlet turned to the king. 'Is this true?' he asked. 'Have you been poisoning me?'

''Tis is an outrageous slander,' said the king, 'that shall not go unpunished.'

'Poison isn't normally something people administer in one dose,' said Selby. 'They give lots of small doses over a long period of time. Your family all eat together. That would be easy to do. Think about it. When you visited my world, you said all the food tasted so much better. Perhaps that's because someone has been putting hebenon in your food here.'

'So you have you been driving me to this insanity?' accused Hamlet, turning on his uncle.

'Not I,' said the king. 'Your addled brain is entirely of your own making. There is no proof for these outlandish, treasonous claims.'

'Fine,' said Selby. 'If I'm totally wrong, then drink from that cup.' She pointed to the cup that the king had placed at the front of the table for Hamlet.

The king looked at the goblet. 'This is a trick,' he protested. 'You poisoned the cup to implicate me.'

'I haven't been anywhere near that cup,' said Selby. 'You poured the wine and offered it to Hamlet.'

'Drink,' said Hamlet. 'If you have nothing to hide, drink.'

Everyone in court was watching. No-one was coming to the king's defence.

'This is all nonsense,' said the queen. She did not want to believe badly of her son or her husband. 'I will drink it,' she said, snatching up the cup.

The king looked horrified, 'Gertrude!'

'No, mother,' cried Hamlet.

'Don't!' pleaded Selby.

But the queen took a deep draught.

'Mother?' cried Hamlet, rushing to her.

The guards used the opportunity to come forward and seize Selby, but she barely noticed. She was watching the queen. Hamlet's mother seemed fine . . . for a moment. But then the queen started to grow uncomfortable, and then distressed.

'Mother are you well?' asked Hamlet.

'No, no,' said the queen. She looked at the goblet in her hand. Hamlet took it from her and put it back on the table. 'The drink, the drink – o, my dear Hamlet. I am poisoned.'

Hamlet held his mother as she collapsed in his arms. She struggled to keep breathing for a few more moments, but then – she was dead.

'Oh, villainy!' cried Hamlet, pressing his mother's face to his own. He gently laid her down, then turned on his uncle. 'Treachery!'

'Oh, yet defend me, friends,' pleaded the king, but no-one moved to help him.

Hamlet leapt up and grabbed the king by the neck. He picked up the cup and held it to the king's mouth. 'Here, thou incestuous, murderous, damned Dane, drink off this potion!' ordered Hamlet. 'Is thy union here? Follow my mother.'

The king tried to resist, but Hamlet forced him to take the drink in his mouth. The king spluttered but couldn't help but swallow some. Hamlet kept pouring more into his mouth. The king swallowed and was soon clutching at his throat. He gurgled and wretched, trying to spit it back out, but it was too late – the poison had taken its grip. The king clutched his throat as it contracted, starving oxygen from his heart and collapsed immobile on the ground at Horatio's feet – his face a hideous purple mask of death.

'The king is dead,' said Horatio.

'Nay, that murderer t'was never a king,' said Hamlet. 'He was a devil deceiving us all.'

'He is justly served,' said Laertes.

Hamlet sank to his knees beside his mother. He picked up the cup again. 'Heaven make thee free of it! I follow thee,' he said, bringing the cup to his own lips.

'No,' cried Selby, running over and smacking the cup out of his hands. The poison spattered across the floor. Courtiers leapt out of the way as if the liquid could hurt them by splashing on their legs. 'You are the King of Denmark now!' said Selby, grabbing Hamlet by the collar and looking into his eyes. 'Your mind will clear. You will think rationally again in a few days when the poison is cleared from your body. Have faith in yourself. Hold strong.'

Outside, they could hear the sound of trumpets.

'What does this fanfare herald?' asked Hamlet.

A courtier hurried forward. 'Young Fortinbras, with conquest come from Poland,' the courtier explained. 'To the ambassadors of England, he gives this warlike volley.'

Hamlet turned to his mother. Her eyes were glassy and her skin was pale. Her last expression, a look of horror, was frozen on her contorted face as she lay dead. 'Good night, sweet queen,' murmured Hamlet. 'And flights of angels sing thee to thy rest.' He kissed her forehead.

The sound of drumming was getting closer.

The doors were flung open and Fortinbras entered. He looked young and splendid in his military uniform. On seeing the room, he baulked.

'What is this sight?' asked Fortinbras, shocked to see the king and queen both dead.

Hamlet laid his mother down tenderly and rose to his feet. 'The queen was poisoned by her husband's hand,' explained Hamlet. 'Her love for him was too great for her to believe that he had done so. And he met justice with the same cup.'

There was a pause where no-one seemed to know what to say or do. Fortinbras was a triumphant general from Norway. His entire army was right outside the castle. What happened in the next moments would decide the fate of Denmark. If Fortinbras denounced Hamlet, he would be dethroned and executed.

Selby knew she had to do something. She called out in a clear voice, 'All hail Hamlet, King of the Danes!'

This galvanised the crowd of courtiers and attendants into action. They responded in kind. 'Hail! Hail! Hail!'

Fortinbras came forward and bowed to Hamlet.

Selby felt a tugging at the back of her sweater.

She turned. Dan was behind her. 'What are you doing here?' she asked.

'Come on, it's time to go,' whispered Dan. He took her hand and drew her back towards the curtain.

'But it's all still a mess,' said Selby.

'The fifth act is resolved,' said Dan. 'The story has come full circle.'

'We couldn't save the queen,' said Selby. She had tears in her own eyes. She had liked the queen, despite her faults. Selby looked back at the horrible scene.

Dan shook his head sadly. 'In stories, if you commit a sin, you must pay a price. The queen may not have known that she had married her husband's murderer, but she did. That is an irredeemable sin in folklore. In can only be absolved by a virtuous death. She got that. This is the best end she could have.'

'It's all so violent,' said Selby.

'Not as violent as it was,' said Dan. 'Hamlet survived. Laertes too. And Ophelia, as well as Rosencrantz and Guildenstern. This is a better ending.'

'What would Shakespeare think?' asked Selby.

'It doesn't matter,' said Dan. 'He's been dead for four hundred years. It wasn't his story to start with anyway. Shakespeare took the story from even more ancient folklore and changed it to suit his times. Now you've lifted your story from his. That's how story-telling works – it's rewritten and retold to make sense to each generation. But the kernel holds true through the ages. Come on.'

Dan led her back towards the drapery. Selby glanced back for one last look at Hamlet. He was shaking hands with Fortinbras. They were much the same age. The tableau looked right.

Dan opened their copy of *Hamlet*. Selby looked down at the words on the page. 'Who knew words could have so much power,' she muttered.

'Read us home,' said Dan.

Selby took the play and she read . . .

FORTINBRAS . . . *Take up the bodies.*
Such a sight as this becomes the field,
but here shows much amiss.
Go, bid the soldiers shoot.

17

Full Circle

A s they were drawn into the book, they could
hear the crackle of cannon fire behind them
in the castle. They were falling through words and
phrases . . .

> . . . *To be, or not to be . . .*
> . . . *What a piece of work is man . . .*
> . . . *Madness in great ones must not unwatched*
> *go . . .*
> . . . *Conscience doth make cowards of us all . . .*
> . . . *When sorrows come, they come not single*
> *spies but in battalions . . .*

Then Selby heard her own voice. It was distant as

if she was speaking aloud to an audience in a theatre. She heard herself say . . .

> *'Absent thee from felicity awhile,*
> *And in this harsh world draw thy*
> *breath in pain,*
> *To tell thy story.'*

With those last words ringing in her ears, Selby tumbled head first onto the floor of the shop. She was so exhausted she just lay there for a moment. It was actually nice to smell the carpet. It smelled like home.

Selby turned sideways, so she could see through the shop window. It was dark outside.

'Are you okay?' asked Dan.

Selby pushed up from the ground onto her hands and knees. Dan was getting to his feet a few metres away.

'Not really,' said Selby.

'You did so well,' said Dan.

'But what did I do?' asked Selby. 'They were fictional characters. But they were real. And all that violence. It's not like in the movies. Or at a play. It was all so real. The horror in the queen's eyes. Polonius's blood – when it got on my hand – it was warm.'

'You helped them,' said Dan. 'You helped make sense of it all. I don't know why you had to do it, but you did it. And that's what matters.'

'All this has done is put me off reading books more than ever,' said Selby. A tear started to run down her face, then another and another.

'Oh no,' said Dan. 'There's no going back now. You have a gift. You can't get away from that.'

'I hope the next thing we study for English is more gentle,' said Selby, laughing between sobs. 'Something where nothing happens, like Jane Austen.'

'No such luck,' said Dan with a smile. 'You've got Ms Karim and you're in year 10.'

'So?' asked Selby.

'Next term you're studying *King Lear*,' he grinned.

'Is that a messy one too?' asked Selby.

'You'll see,' said Dan. 'I don't want to ruin it for you.'

Dan reached out and gave Selby a hug. She hugged him back. They had been through so much together. It felt like an eternity since he'd first stepped into the bookstore and announced he was her tutor.

'What are you two doing now?' demanded Mum.

Dan quickly let Selby go. She toppled backwards into the biography section.

'I thought you were meant to be studying!' said Mum. 'Is it really too hard for you to sit and work for just one hour.'

'Selby has been working hard, Mrs Michaels,' said Dan. 'After just two days, she now has a deeper understanding of *Hamlet* than anyone else I know.'

'And this involves hugging, does it?' demanded Mum.

'We were re-enacting the queen's death scene,' said Selby. She looked so serious and she still had tears in her eyes, it made Mum pause. Although she was still sceptical.

'Really?' said Mum. 'Tell me – what is *Hamlet* about then?'

Selby thought for a moment, trying to order her ideas into words. 'Loss. Grief,' she said eventually. 'It's about being full of emotions and feelings that no-one understands. It's about not knowing what to do, and not feeling brave enough to do what needs to be done. It's a play about broken people making bad choices and ruining the lives of everyone around them. It's about indulging in words when you should be taking action. It's about self-absorption. And Hamlet's self-absorption is really a self-portrait of Shakespeare's own self-absorption in the wake of his son's death.'

'You actually read it!' said Mum.

'Bits of it,' said Selby. 'We watched other bits get acted out.'

Mum burst into tears.

'Why are you crying?' asked Selby.

'I'm just so grateful that you finally read a book,' said Mum. Now she was wrapping Selby in a hug.

'It's not a book,' said Selby. 'It's a play. And a play is just a story. I've always liked stories. I'm just not as good at reading as most people, so I find them easier to enjoy when they're on the television.'

'But when words are written down and you create the meaning from your own imagination, it's so much more profound,' said Mum.

'I'm not like you and Dad, or Eric or Amanda,' said Selby. 'My brain doesn't work the same way. Reading is hard for me. The words on the page don't translate into my head the way they do for other people. I'm never going to read like the rest of you.'

'But if you try,' said Mum, 'it will get easier. You'll get better.'

'Mum, listen to yourself,' said Selby. 'You're like one of those athletic parents who can't handle the fact that one of their kids isn't good at sport.'

'But you're not good at sport either,' said Mum. 'You don't read. You don't play sport. You don't draw. You don't play an instrument. What are you good at? What is your passion?'

Selby couldn't speak. She had a lump in her throat so big she didn't think she could get any words out, even if she did know what to say.

'That isn't fair,' said Dan. 'Selby is brilliant.'

Selby assumed Dan was joking, but when she looked at him, she realised he wasn't.

'Really?' said Mrs Michaels.

Dan nodded. 'She has a true moral compass. It guides her through the complexity of the language in *Hamlet* and so she can see it for what it is – a man under enormous pressure behaving badly,' he said. 'She understood the play better than me.'

Mrs Michaels dabbed a tear from her eye. 'You two must have had quite the tutoring session.'

'We did,' agreed Selby.

'Reading is important,' said Dan. 'But stories are even more important, because stories are the patterns that make humans tick. Selby gets that better than anyone I've ever known. You should be proud of her.'

'I am,' said Mrs Michaels. 'I wish I had a more tangible reason for it.'

'Hamlet was diabolical,' said Selby, 'but his mother still loved him. At least I'm not diabolical. I haven't stabbed anyone with a sword.'

'I am grateful for that,' said Mrs Michaels. She blew her nose loudly on a tissue. 'We'll just have to get you to stop throwing rocks at echidnas.'

'You know I didn't do that, right?' said Selby.

Mrs Michaels smiled. 'But we're never going to stop teasing you about it. It's such a good story.'

Selby kissed her mum on the forehead. She knew she was as tall as her mother, but this was the first time she had felt the same height.

'You'd better run along home,' Mum said to Dan. 'Your dad will have your dinner ready.'

'I've just got to check something in a book first,' said Dan. 'If that's okay?'

'Sure,' said Mrs Michaels. 'I'll leave Selby to lock up.'

Mum took the account ledgers upstairs to the apartment while Dan disappeared down the aisle with the classics.

'What are you doing?' Selby asked.

'I wanted to check that Hamlet's happy ending stuck,' said Dan.

Dan took a new copy of *Hamlet* off the shelf and flicked to the last page. But then he looked up at Selby – offering her the book. 'Do you want to read it?'

'You'd better do it,' said Selby. 'If I start reading, who knows where we'll end up and I've had enough of Denmark for today.'

'Fair enough,' said Dan. 'Okay, let's see . . .' He scanned the page. 'Act five, scene two. The stage directions say Fortinbras places the crown upon Hamlet's head.'

'That's great!' said Selby. 'What did Hamlet say?'

'The last line is . . .' said Dan, 'For me, with sorrow, I embrace my fortune.'

Selby thought about this. 'That's good. It's restrained and appropriate. Maybe the poison was wearing off.'

'And he didn't stab anyone,' said Dan.

'That's definitely an improvement,' said Selby.

Dan smiled at Selby. She looked into his eyes. Really looked. She felt like she was falling into his sadness the same way she had fallen into the play. She dropped her eyes to the floor.

'You better get home to your dad,' said Selby. She went over to the door, unlocked the deadlock and held it open for Dan.

But as he passed through, Dan paused. 'Are you all right?' he asked.

'Not really,' said Selby. 'But I will be. I think.'

Dan nodded. He looked like he wanted to say something but couldn't find the words. He settled for, 'See you next week, then.'

Selby froze with the door still in her hand. 'What for?'

'We'll be starting on *King Lear*,' said Dan.

'I don't think I can handle doing this again!' said Selby.

'Of course you can,' said Dan. 'Reading is good for you.'

The end

Need Help?

If you're going through a tough situation that you don't feel comfortable talking about with your friends or family, you can find help elsewhere. Reach out to a counsellor on a free anonymous hotline or website.

AUSTRALIA
Kids Helpline: 1800 55 1800 / kidshelpline.com.au
Free, private and confidential 24-hour phone and online counselling service for young people aged 5 to 25. You can call any time, for any reason.

NEW ZEALAND
0800 What's Up: 0800 942 8787
Mon–Sun 11am–11pm / whatsup.co.nz
Free counselling helpline and webchat service for children and teenagers.

HAVE YOU READ FRIDAY BARNES?

R. A. Spratt
FRIDAY BARNES
Girl Detective

R. A. Spratt
FRIDAY BARNES
Under Suspicion

R. A. Spratt
FRIDAY BARNES
Big Trouble

R. A. Spratt
FRIDAY BARNES
No Rules

R. A. Spratt
FRIDAY BARNES
The Plot Thickens

R. A. Spratt
FRIDAY BARNES
Danger Ahead

R. A. Spratt
FRIDAY BARNES
Bitter Enemies

R. A. Spratt
FRIDAY BARNES
Never Fear

R. A. Spratt
FRIDAY BARNES
No Escape

R. A. Spratt
FRIDAY BARNES
Undercover

R. A. Spratt
FRIDAY BARNES
Last Chance

About the Author

R.A. Spratt was born in the UK and lived in Dursley, Gloucestershire – a town immortalised by Harry Potter's deeply unpleasant relatives – until she was two years old. Then, like many ambitious English people cursed with regional accents so strong no other British person can take them seriously, her family moved to Australia.

The tedium of growing up in the western suburbs of Sydney was fertiliser to the growth of R.A.'s imagination. The only thing for a kid to do was get on a bicycle and go to the library, so R.A. Spratt did just that. Once there, she read everything, devouring the books of Arthur Ransome, Enid Blyton, Roald Dahl, Robin Klein and Judy Blume, and audiotapes of Shakespeare productions and Sherlock Holmes dramatisations. And so, her young mind was formed, and set on the path of becoming the extraordinary author she is today.

Now based in Bowral NSW, she's the bestselling writer of dozens of absurd and witty books including Friday Barnes, The Adventures of Nanny Piggins, The Peski Kids and the *Shockingly* and *Astonishingly Good Stories* collections. Her podcast, *Bedtime Stories with R.A. Spratt*, has had over 2 million downloads and connects R.A. with story-lovers across the globe.

For more information, visit raspratt.com